"We should be friends...with benefits."

Zac nuzzled her ear. "What do you think?"

Chris sat there stupidly for two seconds. This was exactly what *she* wanted. She was ridiculously hot for him and wanted his body immediately.

"Sweetheart." He leaned in a couple of inches closer.

"Mmm?"

"It's up to you to move away if you want. Because I'm going to kiss you."

"Oh my." Chris stared at his spectacular mouth. She could practically taste it again. "That sounds like a terrible idea."

"It gets worse." He leaned toward her until his amazing lips were brushing her sk slowly turning her molten. "Because if I kiss going to want to stop there."

"Oh! That *is* worse. M imagining his ha warm torso lowerin r behind hers. Or—

His mouth tas ul as it had the other night, an e of his lips ignited a fierce and primar se in her. Chris wanted this. She'd invited this. And the passion that came to life between them, her legs locking around his, their hips straining toward each other?

Oh yes, they could be friends...but bring on those benefits.

FEB 1 2 2015

3 1133 07483 2967

Dear Reader,

I had such a great time writing my recent Blaze story *Some Like It Hotter*, the story of the free-spirited and quirky Eva Meyer, and her determined pursuit of Ames Cooke that upends his world. But when I came to write *The Perfect Indulgence* about Eva's twin sister, Chris, I wasn't quite sure what kind of man to pair her with.

Then I stumbled over Zac Arnette. He and Chris are alike in many ways. Being an engineer, Zac is precise, methodical and controlled. But I gave him all this simmering sexual energy under the surface and an amazingly intuitive side. All I had to do then was introduce him to Chris and watch him fall madly in love, not with the woman Chris thinks she has to be, but with the woman she really is.

Who doesn't want that? If I wasn't happily married, I'd want to give Zac a call myself.

Happy reading!

Isabel Sharpe

IsabelSharpe.com

Isabel Sharpe

The Perfect Indulgence

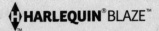

Recycling programs
for this product may
not exist in your area.

ISBN-13: 978-0-373-79836-0

The Perfect Indulgence

Printed in U.S.A.

Isabel Sharpe was not born with pen in hand like so many of her fellow writers. After she quit work to stay home with her firstborn son and nearly went out of her mind, she started writing. After more than thirty novels for Harlequin, a second son and eventually a new, improved husband, Isabel is more than happy with her choices these days. She loves hearing from readers. Write to her at isabelsharpe.com.

Books by Isabel Sharpe

HARLEQUIN BLAZE

While She Was Sleeping...
Surprise Me...
Turn Up the Heat
Long Slow Burn
Hot to the Touch
Just One Kiss
Light Me Up
Feels So Right
Half-Hitched
Back in Service
Nothing to Hide
Some Like It Hotter

Visit the Author Profile page at Harlequin.com for more titles

1

BREATHE IN…BREATHE OUT…breathe in…breathe out.

Chris Meyer sat on a cliff near Aura Beach in her adopted town of Carmia on the Central California coast. She was meditating, in a deep trance, aware only of the breeze on her face, the sounds of the ocean waves rolling in and the slow pattern of her breathing.

If anyone had told her a little over five months ago when she and Eva, her sister and fellow coffee-shop owner, had first cooked up the idea of temporarily switching lives, that she would someday practice meditation, she would have laughed and assumed the person had confused her, a typical type A New Yorker, with her laid-back California-girl twin.

However, in the past five months Chris had undergone a total personality transformation, thanks to her daily meditation and yoga classes at the Peace, Love and Joy Center on the outskirts of town. Gone were her uptight, neurotic and anal-retentive tendencies; she was now relaxed, carefree and brimming with California sunshine and roses.

Most of the time.

Back in October, if someone had suggested she sit

on a cliff for half an hour doing absolutely nothing, she would have scoffed. What could possibly be considered productive about that?

She'd learned so much living here. And with Eva's serious boyfriend, Ames Cooke, so far unsuccessful at finding the perfect sales-manager job with a vineyard or distributor here in Central California, Chris wouldn't be switching back to the hectic pace of New York anytime soon.

That was good. She wanted to stay here until this change went much deeper than her surroundings. Much deeper than her new casual wardrobe, her new crazy hairstyles— Well...actually, they were wigs and temporary hair dyes she'd been experimenting with, but that counted as change, right? Deeper than her new phoenix tattoo, which, admittedly, was tiny and hidden on her rib cage under her arm. And deeper than the row of earrings she'd taken to wearing down the shell of her ear. Although, truth be told, they were cuffs. She didn't want any more holes in her ears. But this was a true transformation. Really. She was going for total calm, ready to say goodbye to the high-strung, anxious, quick-to-judge side of her personality. She was also working on freeing her spontaneous, live-in-the-moment self from a lifetime spent planning, organizing and following routines, which she'd learned from her parents. When she and Eva had been infants, their parents had put them on strict feeding schedules. As girls, they'd been taught the importance of doing their chores and getting a full eight hours of sleep. For whatever reason their parents' devotion to work before play had not remotely rubbed off on her free-spirited twin, but Chris had bought into it 100 percent.

The ringing of her cell phone wrenched her from her trance. She'd forgotten to put the pesky device on mute.

If she could, she'd leave the phone at home when she meditated, but she was responsible for anything that happened at Slow Pour, her sister's coffee shop, which Chris had been managing over the fall and now into winter.

Winter…ha! Californians shouldn't be allowed to use the term.

The call was from Eva. Chris answered eagerly, not having spoken to her sister in a while, unusual for them. "Hey, twin, what's going on? How are you liking February?"

Eva groaned. "Given that it's the first of the month, about as much as I loved January."

"Yeah, it's bitter here, too. *Brr.* I think it might have dipped below sixty."

"*Do not* even tell me."

"You're a traitor to your Wisconsin roots." Chris smiled, knowing better than to push further, since she'd been on the receiving end of this same teasing from Eva for years. "How's my baby doing?"

"Good! You might not know it, but NYEspresso is hosting a fabulous Valentine's event in two weeks. You're having a pastry chef in for the day to give lessons on making heart-shaped meringues and those hot chocolate cakes with the gooey centers."

"Ooh, yum. I am truly brilliant."

"What am I doing at Slow Pour to celebrate the beautiful day of lovers?"

"Oh, I ordered some heart-shaped vegan whole-grain cookies."

"And…?"

"That's it right now." She felt vaguely guilty, since her sister loved the holiday that Chris found forced and silly. Her two previous serious boyfriends had felt the same way, so she'd gotten used to ignoring it. But maybe as part of her new persona, she should be more open to Valentine's Day, even if it was a manufactured occasion designed to profit florists, jewelers, restaurants and chocolate makers. "I might offer a special flavored cocoa drink or something…"

"Are you okay? You don't sound happy, Chris."

"What?" Her sister's comment surprised her, and then she realized Eva still couldn't understand her recent vow to be single and work on her inner self for a change. "No, I'm happy. Deeply happy, as a matter of fact."

Eva gasped. "Really? Does this have to do with the regulars you've met at the shop? Has Gus grown up and gotten smart enough to take you on a decent date instead of out to watch him surf? Has Bodie stopped admiring his hot self long enough to come in and say hello again? Have you started something with my best friend, Zac? Or is there someone new now?"

"No, nothing like that." Chris cringed at the verbal onslaught. Her sister could use a few sessions at the Peace, Love and Joy Center. Chris's four weeks there had changed her life. "Can't I be happy without a man?"

"Of course you can! But who isn't happier with one?"

Chris stretched her arm up toward the sun. Her sister was so blissfully in love with Ames that she couldn't see past coupledom as the source of true contentment, while Chris had discovered that true contentment could only come from within. "I'm not focusing on that part of my life right now."

"*What?* I thought you were going to have a wild fling while you're in California."

"I was. I still might. But I'm not going to force it. If it happens, it happens. Right now I'm working on just being."

"Just being what?"

"Just *being*, Eva."

"What the—" Her twin made a sound of exasperation. "Has someone been feeding you funny-tasting brownies?"

"No! I mean, if the perfect guy comes around and my inner voice tells me to go for it, I'll go for it. But I'm not looking. I'm trying to live in the moment, to be at peace with myself."

"Uh-huh. Hey, listen, can you put my sister on the phone, please? Chris Meyer? Type A, from New York?"

"Ha-ha. You've always let life take you where it wanted, Eva. And look how happy you are. Now I'm trying it."

"But that's who I am, Chris. And when it comes to men, hell, I've always gone after them with everything I have. Poor Ames didn't stand a chance."

"If I meet someone that wonderful, I might do that. Right now, though, sex is not on my mind. Besides, Gus and Bodie have been away forever at surfing events all over the country."

"And Zac disappeared. I told you about that. His younger brother got into some trouble."

"I'm not interested in Zac."

"So you keep saying."

Ordinarily Chris would have gone nuts over Eva's stubborn insistence on believing what she wanted to be true, instead of what was. She would have argued and protested, trying in vain to use logic and common sense to counteract Eva's crazy assumptions. But now… "Okay, whatever, Eva."

"Listen, I wanted to tell you that it looks like a sales-manager job is opening up at Great Grapes Wine Distributors."

A tiny shiver of dread mixed with Chris's pleasure at

hearing her sister's news. If Ames got the job, she'd have to go back to New York before she was ready. She wasn't quite sure what being ready entailed, but she knew if she had to leave soon, something would be left undone here. Going back now would prevent her from achieving the depth of meaning or happiness that she was meant to find or figure out in California.

"That would be perfect for Ames. It's only a half hour from here."

"I know!" Eva squealed. "Shh, don't jinx it. But it would be awesome."

"It would." Chris took a deep breath. Her old self would have panicked immediately. Now she gently told herself that many things would have to happen before Ames and Eva actually moved back here and she had to return to New York. Thinking about it now—worrying and working herself up into an awful state of *what-if*— served no useful purpose.

But up here on the cliff, overlooking the ocean that stretched to eternity, she didn't feel quite one with the universe anymore. Which was fine. She'd go back to Slow Pour a little early and give Summer, the shop's other barista, a shortened shift. Summer worked hard; she deserved an extralong afternoon off, especially since Maureen, their usual weekend barista, had flown out of state to attend a family funeral.

Back at Slow Pour there was a decent crowd for early afternoon on a weekend. Chris would like to think the small changes she'd made to the shop—with Eva's permission, of course—had helped business. She'd drastically reduced the number of non-food-related items for sale, retaining only those with local ties or that sported the shop's logo. In addition, she'd toned down the decor, removing some of the more brightly colored art pieces and several photos of her and Eva as kids at coffee plantations they'd visited with their coffee-scientist father. The result was a classier feel with better feng shui and more room for tables, as well as improved curb appeal to lure in people who were just driving through town.

Of course, she'd left the surfboard menu hanging over the counter. Chris wasn't going to mess with something so sacred.

"You're here early." Summer beamed at Chris, looking radiant as usual, her teeth stunningly white, skin flawless and golden-blond hair a wavy mane she wore pulled back into a ponytail—the quintessential California girl. She was also, as Chris had found out, extremely smart and totally reliable. Plus she pulled one hell of a shot of espresso.

"I know." Chris went behind the counter and headed toward the back office. "I thought I'd give you a whole two hours of paid vacation this afternoon."

"Wow, really?" Summer's light brown eyes lit up. "That would be great."

"Yeah?" Chris grabbed her blue-and-white Slow Pour apron from the row of hooks outside her office. "You have fun plans?"

"Oh, no, not really. It's just nice to get extra time off."

Chris nodded, wondering why such a pleasant and attractive woman seemed to have no social life—at least, none she ever spoke of. Chris should give her time off more often. It was such a small thing, and spreading happiness and good vibes was rewarding for all concerned. "You're welcome. Enjoy the time."

A few customers came in as Summer was leaving, which kept Chris busy for a while, after which she had time to stand back and soak in the atmosphere. Old Chris would have been studying sales reports, worrying about how to improve business, brainstorming new blends, drinks and special bakery items. Now she just wanted to reflect on what she and her sister had created here, and bask in how the café was bringing so much pleasure to its customers and to the community.

A familiar figure caught her eye, winding through the outside tables, heading for the shop's front door.

Zac Arnette.

Chris's heart sped up and her breath hitched. Immediately she relaxed her shoulders and closed her eyes as she took a long, healing breath. Zac had been away for a long time and now he was back. There was no reason for her to be anxious.

Zac was one of Eva's best friends—in fact, they'd had a half-serious pact to get married if neither of them found anyone else by the time they turned thirty—but she personally found him overbearing and bossy and, at times, infuriatingly smug. He'd get an amused look on his face, as if he *loved* that she was struggling, *loved* that he'd gotten to her. It made her *so*—

Ahem.

Not to be blaming him for who he was, of course. She accepted that. She accepted her physical reaction to him, didn't fight it, didn't blame herself for it, even though she didn't really understand why she reacted the way she did.

"Hello." She smiled peacefully, aware of a few butterflies still trying to wreak havoc in her belly.

"Hello, Chris." His blue eyes were warm and the butterflies started fluttering harder. Which was perfectly natural. Zac was a very handsome man. Too surfer blond for her taste—she liked dark East Coast guys with high energy and sharp edges—but…yes, very handsome. He looked a little like the guy who played Thor in the movies, but more real, less model perfect. Very, very handsome.

"You've been away awhile." To her surprise, her tone was tinged with bitterness. Immediately she smiled more brilliantly to take away any impression that she cared that he'd disappeared for months without saying a word to her, although he'd filled Eva in extensively and often on the reason for and progress of his trip.

Which was fine. This wasn't a competition. He had every right to do whatever he wanted. Chris accepted that.

"Family stuff." He came right up to the counter. She'd forgotten how big he was. In her mind, Zac had shrunk to a size that wasn't quite so intimidating. Her lungs were having a little trouble working again, and her heart refused to conform to the peaceful pace she strove to maintain.

Argh! Why did he have to—

No, wait, she *accepted* her own part in this.

"My younger brother, Luke, got into some trouble. I flew east to help him out and brought him back home with me for a while. Why, did you miss me?"

"Oh. No. I don't—" She felt her face flaming. Her jaw clenched. She wanted to smack him. Three months of inner peace shot to hell in two minutes. *Thanks, Zac.*

No, no, no. She wouldn't assign blame. Inner peace was her own responsibility. "I noticed you were gone. Does that count?"

"Sure." He looked smug. Smug! She *knew* he would. And it made her want to smack him harder. "You changed your hair."

"I did." That morning she'd put on a short asymmetrical wig, which she particularly loved because it took her out of her comfort zone, made her look a bit wilder and more unpredictable and helped make her feel that way, too. But with Zac looking at her much too carefully, she only felt exposed as a fake.

So? She wasn't one. Just a beginner at unearthing new feelings and new parts of herself. This was all part of her transformation, freeing herself to explore new potentials. She'd spent too long watching other people really live while she stood sensibly on the sidelines, held there by the weight of her parents' values and expectations.

She refused to care whether Zac liked the new look or not. In fact, she'd let him think it was permanent.

"Nice," spoken with no enthusiasm, still studying her. "Something else has changed about—"

"What can I get you?" She wanted to remind him that their relationship was customer and barista, and he had no place giving opinions on her appearance.

No, wait. He did. He had that right, and she accepted it.

Oh, man. She needed to get back to her cliff.

"How about a tall French roast and…" His blue gaze faltered, then focused on her with renewed intensity, unsettling her further. "And the chance to spend time catching up with you."

Chris blinked. Blinked again. She should be taking cleansing and healing breaths right now.

She wasn't breathing at all.

Was Zac asking her out? No, no, he couldn't be. He hadn't mentioned a place or event. He just wanted to find out what she'd been doing while he was gone. Probably just being polite.

"Well." She turned away to pour his coffee, finding it much easier not to look at him. "It's not busy here now. We can talk."

He didn't answer. Chris turned back, holding out his mug. His eyes pinned her. She felt as if she'd suddenly started moving in slow motion. "Actually, Chris, I meant I'd like to have dinner sometime."

Dinner sometime?

"I…we…you…"

He chuckled—of course he did, her discomfort *always* amused him, the rat—and took the coffee out of her hands. "Think about it."

Chris stepped back, inhaled long and slow through her nose, blew out the tension between her lips, and relaxed her tongue and her shoulders as she'd learned to do. She was free to accept or reject his offer. She had power in this situation. And if he'd get the hell away from her, she could take some time to examine her feelings before she answered, as she'd also learned to do. "Thank you. That's a very nice invitation."

His eyebrow quirked. "Something's different about you. Besides the hair."

"Yes." She did not owe him an explanation.

"Okay, then." He shot her a grin and started toward his usual table, leaving Chris hopelessly trying to get her Zen back.

The door banged open, making her jump and Zac turn. A young, slightly familiar-looking man walked in. Chris glanced at Zac and then back. Was this his younger brother? He was darker than Zac, one eyebrow pierced with a silver ring, slender where Zac was built, light and quick in contrast to Zac's powerful, deliberate movements, but there was some resemblance.

"So *this* is Slow Pour." The newcomer made the announcement as if he was narrating a movie starring himself. A few patrons paused in midconversation to see who had interrupted the café's peaceful vibe.

Zac suddenly looked wary and tired. Chris felt a pang

of sympathy for him. Whatever trouble this kid had gotten into, it had been hard on his older brother.

The kid who must be Luke ambled toward her, eyes alight with mischief and energy. "And you are therefore Chris."

"That's me." She spoke quietly, not sure what Zac had told him, or what role she'd be assigned in the Luke Arnette show.

"Zac, man, you didn't tell me she was totally gorgeous."

Chris suppressed a groan. Luke might look like his brother, but so far he was behaving exactly the opposite. Point in Zac's favor.

"Didn't I?" Zac shrugged mildly. "Guess I forgot."

"Can I get you some coffee? Tea? Suja Juice?" Chris stretched tall, centering herself, trying to radiate kindness and acceptance, and coming up with an attitude closer to dismay. Darn it. She'd thought she was more thoroughly grounded in her new self. Obviously she still had work to do. "Or would you like something else?"

"How about a date?"

Argh, she'd walked right into that one. "How about *coffee*?"

"You want to have coffee with me? That'd be okay." He winked at her. Winked! "Though I was hoping for dinner sometime."

Gee, where had she just heard *that* phrase?

"Luke, dude, back off." Zac shook his head.

"What, am I poaching on your turf?"

Zac's snorted. "Poaching on my *turf*? Who *says* things like that?"

Luke's arrogance dropped as though it had been shattered with a hammer. "Gimme a break, man. This isn't my world."

"So? Just be your own effed-up and charming self." Zac smacked Luke's shoulder, grinning wryly. "You'll get a lot further with the babes that way."

Chris snorted. "Further with the *babes*? Who *says* things like that?"

Zac jerked his thumb. "He does."

"Let me check this out with Chris." Luke stepped forward, leaning against the counter, his blue eyes so like Zac's that Chris had to force herself not to drop her gaze. "Would you like me better if I wasn't trying so hard?"

"Yes. But only about a thousand percent."

"Okay." He opened those eyes puppy wide, his voice rising a few notches. "Will you go out with me? I'll admit I have an arrest record. I beat someone up. He deserved it, though."

"Why don't you start by ordering something?"

"Sure." He scanned the menu written on the surfboard hanging over her head. His lashes were long and dark, eyes shadowed. Some of his mania must be coming from fear and insecurity. She would cut him a break and be kind, though frankly, she wished both Arnette brothers would get out of her store. Life had been so peaceful without Zac around. Though she supposed it was good to realize how far she still had to go before she could confidently return to New York. Her transformation wasn't worth much if she fell back into her old ways every time something stressful happened.

Luke ordered a mocha latte, which she made with whole milk, and she added a free oatmeal flaxseed raisin cookie to welcome him to Carmia, because he looked as though he hadn't eaten in weeks. He and Zac took their coffees over to Zac's regular table while Chris tried to get back to a state of calm, which proved futile because there was a constant buzz inside her, reminding her of Zac's looming presence.

She wanted to ask him if he'd been accepted into any engineering doctoral programs yet, though Eva probably would have said something if he had. He'd taken a leave from his engineering job at a firm in San Luis Obispo to deal with Luke. Obviously the company he worked for valued him a lot if he was able to come and go like that. Apparently he'd worked at the same company through his master's program at Cal Poly, as well. She was curious what his life had been like growing up in Connecticut, and whether Luke had always been a troublemaker and whether—

Stop. Chris yanked her mind back to the present where it belonged, pulled a couple of shots of espresso for a husband and wife biking through Carmia on their way down the coast, and packed up some whole-grain fruit bars for them to take with them.

Another few customers straggled in. She served them cinnamon-flavored organic brown-rice pudding and lattes made with almond milk, glad the place was busy so she could work on pretending Zac wasn't there.

During the next quiet moment, she was about to head back to check on the bathrooms when the front door swished open again.

"I have arrived, victorious!"

Chris swung around, already smiling. Another familiar face had returned. With his tousled dark hair and blue eyes, Gus Banyon was the sexiest surfer dude of all time—except, perhaps, for his equally gorgeous friend Bodie, who had ten more years and twenty more pounds of solid man muscle on him. "Hey, Gus. Welcome back!"

"Whoa, you cut off all your hair. Why'd you do that?"

Gus didn't look any more pleased with her new do than Zac had been. And was even less polite about it.

"It was time for a change. So what did you win this time?" Gus had spent the past few months competing in surfing competitions across the country.

"Better than a win, I got a sponsor!" He raised his muscled arms. "I am the dude!"

"Gus, that is great." Chris couldn't say she understood his world, but she was a little smarter about it than when she'd arrived in October. Having a sponsor meant money, which meant bigger and more important competitions, and, most important, it meant someone truly believed in Gus's talent. "Congratulations! What can I get you? On the house. Suja Juice?"

"Oh, wow, you're stocking that now?"

"I am." She laughed at his shocked expression. "Your favorite."

"Could I have a Berryoxidant?"

"Coming right up."

"All right!" He lifted his hand for a high five and pulled it back at her withering look. She might have settled into the California vibe, but she was still not going to do *that*.

From the small refrigerator behind the counter, she pulled out a Berryoxidant and handed over the attractive red bottle.

"Thank you, my dudess." Gus lifted the bottle reverently. "Apple, orange, strawberry, banana, raspberry, sour cherry, chia seed, flaxseed, baobab and camu camu. Score!"

She watched him chug half of it, then, without having a clue what he was talking about, listened patiently—well, mostly patiently, she was only human—to his description of the individual waves and how he'd handled them. From time to time she was aware of Zac glancing over in her direction. It was hard to block movement in one's peripheral vision, right?

"So anyway, I'm back in town for a couple of weeks, and I was wondering…" He dropped his eyes to the counter. "Do you want to have dinner sometime?"

His voice must have carried because Zac and Luke stopped their conversation and turned. The color rushed to Chris's cheeks. Fabulous. Month after month blush-free and now three times in one afternoon? What was in the air today? And what was with the phrase *dinner sometime?*

"Oh, Gus. That would be…" She wasn't sure what it would be. Honestly, she'd gotten so used to her peaceful, carefree life that she hadn't adequately planned for what she'd do when Gus came back. They'd gone out on one not-so-great date before he left, though she'd agreed to give him another chance.

But the idea of sitting across from him, listening to wave stories all night…

The door opened. Praying for a barrage of customers so she could get out of answering until she was able to choose the best answer from deep in her always-wise subconscious, Chris glanced over.

Oh, my Lord. Her chance to retrieve any calm out of the afternoon was officially gone.

A serious hunk of man filled the doorway, his hazel eyes meeting hers with such blatant sexuality that she felt a thrill all the way down to her…inner calm. Speak of the handsome devil, it was Bodie Banks, Gus's fellow surfer and mentor. She hadn't seen him for several weeks. He tended to stop in for coffee, smolder for a while and leave. But oh, that smoldering. He was amazing. In a low-down, predatory kind of way, but amazing nonetheless.

"Bodie! My man!" Gus went over, and oh-so predictably there was the skin-on-skin smack of a freaking high five. She wondered if she could give Gus a palmectomy so he couldn't participate in the ridiculous ritual anymore.

Wait. Shh. Those uncharitable thoughts belonged to the old Chris. No living creatures were hurt by high fives; there was nothing wrong with it. Acceptance. Love. Kindness. She was badly off track.

"Hey." Bodie prowled toward the counter, biceps and deltoids popping out of his sleeveless T-shirt, which hung loosely over a pair of bright blue patterned board shorts. "How's it going, Chris?"

Gus fell back a few steps, disciple making room for his master. Zac and Luke continued to watch the spectacle.

Well.

This wasn't at all awkward.

"I'm fine, Bodie. Welcome back to Carmia. What can I get you?" She half expected him to order a cup of whole roasted coffee beans and a spoon. He was that primal.

"Double espresso."

"Coming up." Grateful for the reprieve, she moved back to the gleaming espresso machine, which worked so much more smoothly than hers back in New York. Eva had dubbed her finicky machine the Beast. "So how have you been?" she asked over her shoulder.

"Busy. Too busy. Nice to have a few weeks off now."

"Yeah?" She packed the ground espresso into a solid puck and hooked the portafilter into the machine. "What are your plans?"

"Don't have any. That's the best way to live. Moment to moment. Know what I mean?"

Finally, someone who spoke her new language. She smiled over her shoulder while the machine buzzed. A few months ago, she would have been horrified, imagining that a lack of planning would automatically equal chaos. Now she embraced the concept wholly. Lately, she'd even been doing crazy-impulsive things, like taking walks when it was dinnertime. Just because she felt like it!

Yeah, okay, she was still a beginner when it came to the whole spontaneous thing.

"So, Chris…"

Something in Bodie's tone made her body tense and her heart skip a beat. The espresso machine shut off abruptly, thrusting them into silence.

"Yes?" She picked up the cup and turned to find Zac, Luke and Gus still watching.

Argh!

"Since I'm back and free for a while…" He put both hands on the counter and leaned forward. His muscles bulged, his eyes held hers.

Chris swallowed. *Holy—*

"I'm thinkin' you and me have something pretty powerful between us."

The counter?

She couldn't get the joke out. She was swimming in a sea of hormones and freaking out. In her hands, his espresso cup rattled against its saucer before she could make her hand relax.

"Huh." That was the best she could do. This mental meltdown was not okay—this was no longer who she was, and this was not where or how she wanted to be.

"So I was wondering—" he reached over and touched her cheek, making her skin tingle and causing her to nearly drop the cup "—if you wanted to have dinner sometime."

2

If one more guy asked Chris out, Zac was going to get up from his table at Slow Pour and land an uppercut to his jaw. Then he was going to punch Gus and Bodie retroactively, because that was the kind of mood he was in.

What the hell? Before the holidays, he'd left for Connecticut, where he and Luke had grown up, because Luke was in trouble—again. Zac had wanted to try to set his little brother on a straighter path, but he'd also needed to get away from Chris, to get over himself and stop the stupid mooning.

Nice idea. Didn't work. In Connecticut he'd discovered he could moon long-distance just as easily as he could in California, plus he was reminded of how much he didn't like winter. He'd gone through that misery annually growing up, and he didn't want to do it again.

So he'd come back. Luke needed a change of scenery, needed to get away from his substance-abusing East Coast friends to live a cleaner, better life under his brother's watchful eye.

Luke had been a little surprise package who'd come into the world a week before Zac turned twelve. Three years later, when Luke was a toddler and Zac was in his first year of boarding school, their mother had succumbed to cancer. Their father had done his best to raise Luke on his own since then.

Losing their mother had sucked, to put it mildly. Zac had done most of his grieving on his own while he was away at school. Their already distant father hadn't been in any shape to be a good parent, so Luke bore the worst of the tragedy. Zac had done what he could to help when he was home, but that wasn't often. He had two regrets in life: one, that he hadn't been there more for both Luke and his father, and two, that he hadn't made a pass at Cynthia Baumgehen in college the night they were alone in his room.

Today, the minute he'd laid eyes on Chris, in spite of her weird haircut and new piercings, all the feelings he'd spent the past months trying to suppress had come roaring back. Standing there, overwhelmed, he'd remembered his regret over the missed opportunity with Cynthia and had experienced a big what-the-hell moment. So he'd asked Chris out to dinner, only to see her falter and hem and haw. And then he'd had to watch her get the same freaking offer from *three* other guys, including his own *brother*, for God's sake. As if Zac was no different from a delinquent kid and brain-dead surfer meat.

Apparently he was smart not to have made a pass at Cynthia all those years ago. She probably would have turned pale and thrown up all over herself.

And while he was ranting, who or what had taken the spark out of Chris? She was like an overdecorated shell of her former self. Eva told him Chris had taken a month of classes at the Peace, Love and Joy Center. That was fine, and he had respect for the practices of yoga and meditation—many of the Eastern philosophies of life made good practical sense—but he didn't understand why she had to look deflated and blank and suck air before answering a simple question. Chris Meyer was a high-energy, exciting woman. If she was trying to change that about herself, she would only succeed in driving herself crazy.

Well, fine, then, she'd go crazy. He'd stand by and watch. Not his problem.

"Uh, Zac?" Luke sat across the table, Zac's laptop open in front of him. Supposedly he'd been looking for job opportunities in the area, but Zac was pretty sure his brother had also been taking in the three-ring circus unfolding in front of them nearly as intently as he had been.

"What?" He had no idea what his brother had been saying.

"I asked whether you thought Chris would give me a job at Slow—"

"No." Zac closed his eyes, regrouping. *Who* was going crazy? "I mean, I think she has all the staff she needs."

"Uh-*huh*." Luke was looking at him suspiciously. For all the stupidity he'd demonstrated in his own short life, he was annoyingly perceptive about other people's. "So do you think she'd go out with me if I—"

"No."

Luke raised his pierced eyebrow. "You were in a great mood earlier. What the hell happened?"

"Sorry, man." Zac rubbed his chin, glancing over at Chris, who was smiling up at Bodie as if he was her best friend. "I'm just…" *Damn*, that sweet, sunny smile pissed him off. If Chris was going to go for someone besides Zac, at least she could find a guy with a brain and respect for women. Bodie was so in love with himself he had no room for anyone else.

"Oh, *I* get it." Luke had followed his gaze and was now smirking triumphantly. "All is clear to the amazing Luke."

"What are you talking about?"

"Her." He jerked his thumb back over his shoulder toward Chris. "You're into her. And it's driving you crazy that she might be into Mr. Canned Beef over there."

"That's *not* what is bothering me."

"Yes it is. Don't BS me."

Zac took a deep breath. Early on in this intervention, he'd promised his brother total honesty as the only way they could trust each other. He hadn't counted on the promise backfiring like this. "Okay, okay. *Maybe* you're right."

"I'm right."

"You're *right*, fine. Don't push it." He jabbed a finger at his brother. "And *don't* ask her out again."

"Message received." Luke held up his hands in surrender. "Your turf, I get it. I'll stay away. After all, blood is thicker than semen."

"Oh, *jeez*." Zac grimaced. "Do you *have* to say that stuff?"

In spite of his crappy mood, he was glad to see Luke laugh. The self-conscious tough-guy image got hard to take after a while. When Luke smiled he was Zac's kid brother again.

"If it's any consolation—" Luke motioned to Bodie contemptuously "—that guy's got nothing on you."

"Yeah, thanks." The compliment pleased him, but he would've preferred to hear it from Chris.

"So? What are you going to do about it? What's your plan?"

"My plan?" Zac let his hand drop to the table. "I'm going to go back to work, and help you find a job around here, and I'm going to keep you out of trouble."

"Dude. I meant about her."

"Nothing." Zac stood and set his coffee cup on the

tray for used dishes, only slightly gratified when Chris glanced over distractedly. At least she was keeping track of him. "Let's go."

"Nothing?" Luke got to his feet. "What kind of geek strategy is that?"

"Mine." He led the way out of the shop, not looking at Chris again, not wanting to see her going all dewy-eyed over Mr. Canned Beef, as Luke had appropriately named him. That kind of torture Zac could do without. He'd thought he was so smooth asking her for a date. He was never using the phrase *Dinner sometime?* again.

"Are you going to ignore me for the rest of my life?"

Zac made a sound of frustration and stopped among the shaded tables and coffee-sipping patrons outside the store, swinging around to face his brother. "No, no, I'm not. I'm sorry."

Luke peered up at him. "She's got you, huh?"

"I wouldn't say that."

"Liar."

Zac shook his head and kept walking. "You're pissing me off."

"Yeah? Where are we going?"

"Home to pack up dinner, then we're going to the beach to eat it."

"Beach in February. Cool."

"I'll give you about ten days to figure out why I moved to California."

They passed a woman wearing tight jeans and a low-cut top with a push-up bra. Luke turned, lowering his sunglasses for a better look. "Dude, I figured it out already."

THEY'D FINISHED DINNER—Zac in an only marginally better mood—and were sitting next to a bonfire on Aura Beach when Zac's phone rang, making him tense and then instantly exasperated. When was he going to stop hoping that it was Chris calling? Chris texting? Chris emailing? He really needed to figure out a way to get this woman out of his head before he became unhealthily obsessed.

Yeah, probably way too late for that.

He hauled out his phone and broke into a grin when he saw who the caller was. Jackie Cawling, a friend from his years in the Peace Corps, in his late twenties. They'd both been assigned to Kenya and had dated for a year or so—long-distance, since their towns were miles apart. After their assignments ended, they'd realized their attraction had mostly been based on each other's familiarity in a strange land, and they'd parted pleasantly. Jackie was still traveling, had never settled down and probably never would. Every now and then she'd call, occasionally even show up, and then disappear until the next time he heard from her.

"Jackie! Where are you calling from this time? Italy? China? Australia?"

"Much more exotic."

"Bali? Cook Islands? Venus?"

"Even more out there. I'm in Los Angeles. I have a few weeks with nothing to do before I start a job on a llama farm in Peru and I'm sick of the city and craving the mellowness of the Central Coast. Want to see me?"

"Absolutely." He couldn't stop grinning. "You need a place to stay? My brother's here, but he would love to sleep on the couch."

"Hey." Luke was indignant. "She better be totally hot."

Zac covered the phone to whisper, "Incendiary."

"Yeah?" Luke's eyes lit up. "Couch works for me."

"Thanks, Zac," Jackie said. "It'd just be for a day or two. I have a friend with a cabin in the middle of nowhere on the beach just up the coast from you, and I'll want to hang out there and do my hermit thing for a few days. Then I have some buddies I'm seeing in Santa Cruz and blah, blah, blah, on up the coast. I plan to hit Carmia on Saturday. That's the seventh, I think. That okay?"

"That's great."

"Awesome. I can't wait to catch up. You finished your master's yet? Wait, of course you have. Last time we talked you were about done. So, doctorate now? Where are you applying?"

"Stanford, MIT, Columbia and Penn."

"Oh, my—" Her familiar deep laugh made him smile. "What, you're not trying any *good* schools?"

"Nah, wasn't up to it." He leaned back on the blanket, feeling much better. Jackie knew him about as well as anyone did. Kind of hard to play mind games or hang on to fake attitudes living in a remote African village. "So what about you, Jackie? Where have you been? What have you been doing?"

"I'll fill you in when I see you, at great length. In fact, I look forward to staying up all night over cups of coffee the way we used to. However, I need to know now, since I am a gossip slut, is there a potential Mrs. Zac?"

He snorted. "That remains to be seen."

"Ooh, I'll want details."

"Nothing to tell yet. Why, is there a Mr. Cawling?"

"Nope. Only temporary relief now and then for me. I won't get married until I'm too old to travel. Then I'll find you wherever you are and propose."

"That sounds like a deal. I'll see you Saturday, Jackie." He hung up, warmth spreading through his chest, and felt himself finally starting to relax. Jackie was unique: a strong, confident woman, comfortable in her own skin, generous and dedicated to helping make the world a better place. If he had half a brain he'd fall for her instead of being crazy about a woman who had no idea who she was.

At least Jackie's timing was perfect. He could use a friend, and he could definitely use a distraction.

SUMMER WIPED DOWN the counter at Slow Pour, even though it was already clean. Not much going on this morning. A couple of chairs taken, not exactly a rush at the counter. The café was doing well overall, maybe even a little better than when Eva had been here, but there would always be quiet times. Thank goodness.

If you asked her—which no one had and no one probably would—Summer would say that Chris was sorta losing it. She was still *acting* calm, certainly calmer than when she'd arrived back in October, all wound up. It had been fun watching her slowly relax over the next little while under the influence of Central California.

Then she'd discovered the Peace, Love and Joy Center and had made a typical newcomer mistake, thinking she had to totally submerge herself in their let-it-be philosophy, instead of just taking from it what worked for her. It was hard watching Chris's constant struggle to battle her real nature. And also kind of funny, though it wasn't very nice of Summer to think so.

But over the past few days, she'd noticed things starting to slide. Nothing huge, nothing that would interfere with business. Chris had forgotten to clean a portafilter on the espresso machine. She'd left sales paperwork out on the counter. Toilet paper hadn't been reordered until they were nearly out. The type of mistakes Summer would have expected from flighty Eva, but until now Chris had run the shop impeccably.

Summer had a pretty good idea what had unsettled her temporary boss, but as she said, no one was likely to ask her. The benefit of looking like a stereotypical California girl was that people assumed she didn't have a brain in her head and expected little. Which was handy when she wanted to be ignored, and annoying as hell the rest of the time.

She had big plans for her life, though she hadn't told anyone about them. Telling invited scorn, doubt or ridicule. Or worse, polite encouragement that served as a front for total disbelief. Summer wanted to go to college—no, she *was* going to college. Full-time, not just taking one online class at a time the way she was doing now. And then she was going on to graduate school, in psychology. She'd be the first in her family to get an advanced degree. From there, Summer wanted to—was *going* to—become a therapist, to help kids who hadn't grown up in a house with major identifiable drama for which there were already support networks in place, like alcoholism, drugs, physical abuse or mental illness. But for kids like herself, whose parents had just really sucked at child rearing.

But first…she had to be able to afford full-time college. She'd almost been there, had been planning to start in January, and then her car had died, and her flaky sister needed another loan to pay off credit-card debt, and Summer had had to use a chunk of her savings. A frustrating setback. She'd gotten a really nice scholarship from Cal Poly, and the administration had been great about helping her defer matriculation by a year, but she couldn't keep putting it off.

Next fall, she'd make it there for sure.

The door opened. A kid came in, about her age, maybe a year or two older, wearing nearly round John Lennon sunglasses with smoky-gray frames. Very cool. A small shock of attraction hit her and she pushed the feeling away. Good-looking guys came into Slow Pour all the time. She should be used to it by now.

"Hey." He ambled up to the counter, jeans and T-shirt hanging off his wiry frame. "Is Chris here?"

"Not until two." She smiled pleasantly. "Can I help you?"

"Yeah, um…" He took off his sunglasses to reveal blue eyes framed by long black lashes; a silver ring pierced his right eyebrow. Heart-stopping eyes. Big-trouble eyes, the kind that made her feel stupidly flustered. Eyes that, now she thought about it, seemed oddly familiar. "I was looking for Chris."

Uh. Hadn't she just explained that Chris wasn't here? "She'll be here at two. I'm taking the morning shift today."

"Yeah, um…yeah, okay. You said that. Sorry."

"Did you want to leave her a message?"

"No, no. No, that's okay." He laughed nervously. His mouth was full and very sexy. "I'm being a dork, aren't I?"

Summer lifted an eyebrow, not sure how strongly to agree with him. "Don't worry about it."

"I'm Luke." He held out his hand. "Usually I'm very together. Very smooth. Probably the coolest guy you'll ever meet."

She couldn't help a half smile. "Cool Hand Luke?"

"Sorry?"

"Never mind." Obviously his parents didn't watch TV incessantly. Hers practically never left their recliners. Her brother and sister had inherited the same disease. Summer had had it, too, until she reached high school and realized she was going to have to take responsibly for her own life if she wanted to live it differently. "I'm Summer. Did you want me to tell Chris you stopped by?"

"I was wondering if she wanted to come down to the beach with Zac and me. Do you—"

"You know Zac?" Summer adored Zac. If he was closer to her age, and if she had any chance with him, she'd fall madly in love. But he wasn't, and she didn't, so she kept her hormones under control.

"He's my brother."

"Right, of course." No wonder those eyes looked familiar. Luke was considerably younger, thinner and darker than Zac, with a stronger nose, but the eyes were the same. This must be the brother Zac had flown to Connecticut to rescue from whatever mess he'd gotten himself into. "I should have guessed that."

"Yeah, we're like twins. Most people can't even tell us apart. I'm surprised you didn't think I was him when I walked in."

That got a laugh. He was nervous, edgy, carrying around pain, she guessed. The signs were easy to recognize once you knew them. Her sister, Angela, was the same way. Hilarious, but in a way that made you uneasy to be around. "Can I get you some coffee?"

He glanced at his watch. "How about I come back at two and have a cup with you?"

Uh... Summer could handle this type of question easily from strangers—a quick, polite no, thanks—but she had a hard time saying no to Luke. "I'm not really supposed to date customers."

"It's not a date, and because Zac paid last time we were here, technically, I'm not a customer." He shoved his fingers through his longish, ragged hair and shook it back into place. "No big deal. I'm new in town, don't know anyone my age, just thought maybe..."

Summer bit her lip, taken aback by how much she wanted to accept. This kid had apparently been through some tough times and could use a friend. But she wasn't sure how much trouble he'd gotten into, and she wasn't wild about becoming part of his recovery.

"Never mind. Nice meeting you. Tell Chris I stopped by." He tapped the counter and started walking away, trying to look cool but managing only to look too thin and fragile and rejected.

"Wait." She gestured him back before she'd had time to think about what she was doing.

He turned, eyes hopeful. If he'd looked even remotely triumphant, she would have sent him out again, having realized he'd manipulated her. "Yeah?"

"What did you do? What did Zac have to rescue you from?"

"Only myself." He looked younger when he smiled big like that. "I got into a bar fight. I was drinking too much, hanging with the wrong crowd. But I went to therapy and now I'm perfect."

Summer laughed. "Yeah, congratulations on that."

"Change your mind about coffee? I'm harmless. Just looking for a friend."

Summer grinned. She had a thing for damaged guys, had dated a couple, attracted by their need, naively thinking she could help them. But she'd discovered that damaged guys made really poor partners. All their energy went into coping with just being themselves. "No, thanks. But I'll see you around, I'm sure. Carmia's a small place."

"Yeah, maybe some other time." He looked so sweet and hopeful she felt herself softening.

"Maybe."

"Let me know when you're ready. I'm a patient guy."

She doubted that. But she did feel bad for him. She understood loneliness, how it could alter your perception of everything, from how you felt about yourself to how you felt about the weather. And she understood that impulse, when you felt adrift, to latch onto someone who was firmly anchored.

"See ya." Luke backed up a few steps, putting his sunglasses back on. Then he gave her an I'm-so-cool thumbs-up and barely missed bumping into the door on his way out.

Summer smiled, preferring his clumsy moments to the pretentious ones. At least they were real. He was probably the kind of kid she'd be seeing on her figurative couch someday. It wouldn't be bad to talk to him, see if she could figure out what made him tick. It would be like preparation for her university program even without more than a course or two under her belt.

And she could count on Zac to keep him in line if he ever stepped over it.

In the meantime she'd have to forget that he was, in his own cocky and slightly pathetic way, really, really cute. Her life plan included relationships, but she was looking for someone mature, ambitious, respectful, supportive and able to love openly and deeply. Gorgeous and built wouldn't hurt, but it wasn't as important.

Too bad Zac was out of her league. And from what she'd seen of the way he looked at Chris…not likely to change.

But his brother… She turned away from the counter, looking for something to do to keep herself occupied until the next customer came in, still feeling light and fizzy, thinking about the way Luke looked at her, how hard he'd tried to be a tough guy, yet how easily he'd admitted to his flaws and his efforts to fix them.

With Zac's brother she'd have to be careful.

3

"Four totally hot guys asked you out on Monday? In *one* hour?"

"Yes." Chris sat in a half lotus on the rug in Eva's living room, breathing calmly, waiting while Eva shouted the news to Ames—they'd just gotten back to Ames's luxury Manhattan apartment after a movie and late-night dinner. Ames had been a regular at NYEspresso and had tried to go out with Chris before he met Eva and totally changed his idea of the perfect mate.

"I still can't believe it. How many dates did you agree to go on?"

"None."

"What?"

Chris had to pull the phone away from her ear. Her twin lived large in every way. "Well, none *yet*. I mean, they were all right there watching me. It was completely weird."

"Okay, but you didn't actually say no to any of them."

"I barely said anything." She stood, centering herself, trying to distribute her weight evenly. "I think I was in shock."

Her sister giggled. "I'm not surprised. So which hot hunk o' man flesh are you going to start with?"

"Gus." Chris didn't have to see Eva's face scrunched into incredulity to know what she looked like.

"*Gus?* Are you kidding me? No offense, Chris, but I'd pick *any* of the others over Gus, even not ever having seen Luke, who if you ask me shouldn't be in the running because he's a mere babe. I would definitely pick Zac first."

No, not Zac. Chris tipped her head to one side, feeling her neck muscles lengthen and relax. "Gus is a sweetheart."

"He's a sweetheart, yes. A sweetheart with no brain."

Chris grimaced. Eva was sort of right. But around Gus she could hang on to her Zen-like calm. Bodie was too overwhelmingly sexy, Eva was right about Luke being ridiculously young, even younger than Gus, and Zac...

Chris was many things around Zac, but calm never seemed to be one of them. He seemed to push a button that made her revert to her combative, overly judgmental and high-strung former self.

"I owe Gus. We had one pretty awful date when I first moved out here. I promised him a second chance, but he didn't collect until now."

"*Months and months* later. Don't you think that's extremely weird?"

"He's a guy." Chris tipped her head to the other side. Breathe in. Breathe out. "An ambitious surfer who's been busy catching waves. Maybe he's been dating someone else. I don't know, it doesn't really matter to me."

"Wow, Chris, you sound about as excited about this date as someone looking forward to an IRS audit. I'm worried about you."

Chris rolled her eyes. Once again Eva refused to clue

in to her new outlook on life. "No, it will be fun. I'm looking forward to spending time with him."

Eva sighed. "Ames is telling me to butt out."

"Ames is a very smart man."

"When have I ever butted out of anything? If you ask me—"

"I didn't."

"—you are depressed. You really need to start—"

"Depressed?" Chris's head snapped upright; she jammed one hand onto her hip. "Eva, this is nothing like depression. I'm trying for something I've never had in my entire life, total contentment and total confidence in my ability to give up control and just be in the moment."

"I get that." Eva's voice gentled. "Really, I do. It just… doesn't sound like you."

Chris closed her eyes, let her arm drop and recentered her body, trying to maintain mental equilibrium. It occurred to her suddenly that her twin might just be disoriented by the changes. She tried to think how she'd feel if their positions were reversed and Eva started behaving differently. It would certainly be confusing and frightening. Maybe Chris would react negatively, too. "People change, Eva."

"They don't change *that* much. Not fundamentally."

"Trust me, I'm more me than I ever have been." She glanced at her watch, trying to ignore Eva's exasperated snort, though it hurt a little. "I have to go. Gus is picking me up in a couple of minutes."

"*Now?* It must be after ten there."

"What, do I have a curfew?"

"Sorry. I'm sorry. You're just not a late-night person… Right, I know, you're changing. Well, have fun. Don't do anything stupid like fall for him."

"*Om Saha Naavavatu.* If the crystals align, and my chakra bids me to do it, I just might."

"Uh…Chris? You're really scaring me."

Chris's laughter died into dismay. "Eva, I was *kidding*. I don't really talk like that, and I'm not going to fall in love with Gus. Please don't worry about me. I'm really fine."

"But— Oh. Ames is telling me to butt out again. I'll let you go. Have fun."

"Thanks, Eva." Chris hung up, unsettled and anxious—the way she used to be nearly all the time. She and Eva rarely disagreed, especially about anything so personal. Thank goodness she had a weapon against that kind of tension now. Eva would come around when she saw how much freer and happier Chris was in her new skin, and how their relationship would only change for the better. Next time Eva decided she wanted to go out after Chris had already settled into a comfortable chair with a good book or movie, Chris would be all over it instead of declining. Maybe she'd even cut her hair for real at some point.

A peaceful minute later, she was calm again, adjusting her funky wig, smoothing the hem of her casual floral tunic top which she wore over skinny jeans, and remembering the outfit she'd worn on her first date with Gus—a fancy white top, carefully ironed blue linen shorts and matching sandals. For heaven's sake.

This evening would be fun. Casual and playful. Definitely out of the ordinary. On dates in New York, she'd go to a show, a movie, a museum or to any of the thousands of fantastic restaurants. *Ah, New York.*

Tonight she was going to play pool and darts in a bar with Gus and his buddies. Now that she was so much less judgmental, having let go of the fear that required her to be in control at all times, she was open to so many more experiences. She was quite sure she'd love this one.

THREE HOURS LATER, Chris walked back into the house, head pounding, throat hoarse from shouting over the music and over the other people shouting over the music.

She'd hated every minute of tonight.

The pool hall had been loud and full of too-young, weird-looking people, and as much as she tried very hard to love and accept them all, she really wanted most of them to grow up and be quiet and stop drinking so much. A long, hot shower would be a super idea for many of them, too. And maybe a few could give the tattoo parlor a rest after six or seven thousand visits.

Yes, she'd gotten one tiny tat on a particularly fun evening last fall when she'd been out with Summer and the rest of the part-time staff for a meeting that had turned into a bar visit and a trip to the parlor. She and Summer had both gotten tattoos—after Chris insisted on paying. Summer got a tiny rose on the inside of her upper arm. Chris's phoenix was rising from the ashes to signify her new self emerging. Clichéd, but she loved the symbol. At least her tiny delicate bird didn't take up most of her visible skin so it looked as if she'd been rolling in used engine oil.

She pulled off her wig, kicked off her flip-flops and went into the kitchen to gulp a glass of water. Gus had been adorable, entertaining, eager to please, but thank God, finally even he'd had enough and had brought her home, where she'd kept their good-night kiss to a quick, sweet peck and fled, hoping to discourage him from asking her out again.

Weirdly keyed up—annoying since she was exhausted from being up since five-thirty that morning to work the early shift—she wandered around Eva's adorable little house, watered the plants, and finally decided what she really needed to relax after the crowds and brain-pulverizing noise was a long, soul-cleansing walk on the beach.

Five minutes later, wearing black knit capris, waterproof Teva sandals and a pink sweatshirt, with her real hair stuffed under a matching pink New York Yankees cap, she stopped by the table next to the front door and grabbed her little bag containing an electronic whistle and pepper spray. She'd never felt threatened or uncomfortable on Aura Beach, but kids did go there to drink sometimes, and drunk kids could get really stupid.

Outside, the neighborhood was quiet except for the wind through the trees and waves tumbling in the distance. By the time she'd made it to the bottom of the hill and turned onto La Playa Avenue, her body was relaxing, her headache lessening. She sent Slow Pour a silent, affectionate greeting as she passed, and several blocks later turned right onto the path toward the beach. When the scrubby growth under her feet gave way to sand, she stopped to check in with her surroundings and her instincts.

The moon was bright enough not to need the flashlight app on her phone. The beach appeared deserted.

Chris's mouth curved in a smile. How perfect. In New York when she felt caged and restless late at night, her options were the twenty-four-hour gym a few blocks from her house or staying home and dealing with it.

She sighed rapturously and walked toward the waves, reveling in the fresh ocean breeze. The perfect antidote to an evening spent with—

What was that? Her peripheral vision had caught two shadows off to the right at the base of one of the cliffs bracketing the beach. Two people were getting to their feet. With luck she'd disturbed a horny couple making out, not partying guys looking to cause trouble.

Chris unzipped her bag and slipped a hand inside, trying to look unconcerned, hoping the two shapes would head for the path and be gone.

No. They were heading toward her. They both looked male.

She closed her fingers around the pepper spray, adrenaline pumping, telling herself to stay calm, breathe easy, to send out peaceful loving vibes, and hope they were just going to offer to hang out with her and go away when she said no.

One of them shouted something as a wave broke, the rumble and swish of water drowning his words. She couldn't see their faces, but the taller one's lumbering stride looked familiar.

Zac?

And could that be Luke with him?

She didn't relax until they were close enough to tell for sure, which must have been when they could tell for sure who she was, because they went from what had seemed like an ominously relentless advance to smiling and waving.

For heaven's sake.

She rezipped the bag, her heart still pounding like crazy. There was not enough Zen in the world to stay calm during that kind of episode.

"Hey, Chris." Luke was beaming.

Zac looked— Well, as usual she couldn't tell. He was so hard to read. Except when he was being smug. That came through loud and clear.

"You guys came close to being pepper-sprayed." Her voice shook with relief, but she kept her body still, counting on the noise of the waves to cover up the tremor in her words, not wanting the guys to know how badly they'd spooked her. "It's a terrible idea to sneak up on a woman alone at night."

"Hey, we weren't sneaking," Luke said. "We were walking. And we yelled out to you."

"Sorry, Chris. We didn't mean to freak you out." Zac put his hands on his hips, as usual able to see through her attempts at hiding anything.

"No, it's fine. I'm fine." She waved the concern away. "I just came down here to clear my head and to—" *Be alone.*

The words were on the tip of her tongue, but just as she was about to say them, she looked up at Zac, who was looking down at her, his face dim with the moon behind him, and an odd shiver—not unpleasant—passed through her body.

She'd wanted to make it clear that she didn't want him—them—around tonight, but some part of her wasn't entirely sure that was true. And she was supposed to listen to her true inner voice and its needs and to comply, because that wise subconscious part of her knew best.

Darn it.

"I'm beat. I'm going back up to the house." Luke's voice was a little too loud, not quite natural. "I'll see you later."

Zac made a noise that sounded like a suppressed snort. "Sure. You know the way back?"

"Uh-huh. Up to La Playa, then right, then left on Feo Salmuera and home." He waved and walked quickly up the beach, calling out a singsong, "Have *fun*, guys," that was brimming with mischief.

Chris put her hands on her hips. "Zac."

"Chris." He turned back to her, his face catching the

moonlight from a new angle, making him a broad, mysterious masculine form in the half darkness.

That funny, fizzy shiver hit her again. "Were we just rather pointedly left alone?"

"Looks that way. Do you mind?"

As usual, he took her aback with his directness. No, she didn't mind. Yes, she most definitely *did* mind.

And so it went with Zac.

"I came down here to be alone."

"Okay." His voice was quiet, even. She could take lessons from him on staying calm. He acted as if he didn't care one way or another whether she stayed or left.

Not that *she* cared if he cared one way or another whether she stayed or left.

Really.

"How about I go back over by the cliff where Luke and I were talking, and when you're ready to go let me know and I'll walk you home. That way you get your alone time and I won't have to worry about you."

"Oh." She frowned at the ocean. What a thoughtful and sensible solution. She got what she wanted, and he… Well, who knew what he wanted? He had asked her out to dinner three days ago, on Monday, but maybe that was on a whim he now regretted. "Okay."

"Good." He backed up a few steps. "Just wave at me when you want to leave."

"Wait, so that means you'll be staring over here the whole time?"

"Oh, sure. I have binoculars and X-ray glasses. Standard stalker equipment."

She couldn't help but smile. "Serves me right for asking."

He lifted a hand and walked back toward the cliff. Chris wrapped her arms around herself. The farther away

Zac got, the more empty the beach felt—but not in a good way this time. What was her inner voice trying to tell her?

Aw, crap.

"Zac." He kept walking. *"Zac."*

His lumbering form turned back.

She hurried over. "Hey."

"Something wrong?"

"No, no, I just…" She gestured lamely. "I guess I changed my mind about hanging out."

"Okay." Again, he didn't sound either glad or upset. She *should* take lessons. He was that good.

She fell into step beside him as they walked toward the cliff face. "Does anything ever upset you?"

"Why are you asking me that?"

"Because I was wondering that."

"Ha. Yes, of course things upset me sometimes."

"Has anything ever upset you around me, or do you just never show it? Because I've never seen you—"

"Chris." He stopped walking. "Can we start with 'How was your evening? How are things going? What have you been up to for the past few months?'"

"Okay." She stared up at him, wishing she could see his face better. "How was your evening?"

He chuckled and kept walking. "Fine, thanks. Luke and I went running, then we had dinner, watched some TV, got hungry again and brought more food down here."

"How is he doing?"

Zac sat on one side of a blanket spread at the bottom of the cliff, leaving her plenty of room to join him. "He's okay, considering he changed coasts and is starting his life over. Are you hungry?"

"Actually, yes." She dropped down next to him. She was starving. There had been little at the bar that wasn't loaded with cheese or deep-fried or both. "What do you have? Man food, I bet. Cheetos and beef jerky?"

"C'mon, this is California. We brought sushi, papaya and fair-trade chocolate."

"No way." Her stomach growled viciously. Thank goodness the waves were loud enough to cover the sound. "Do I have to high-five you and call you 'dude' to eat it?"

"If you want." He lit a small lantern that threw a warm circle of light onto the sand and their blanket. "But how about you tell me about your evening instead?"

"I went out with Gus."

"Yeah?" Zac's body hitched as he leaned toward the cooler, but his voice stayed even, so she couldn't tell if he'd reacted or not. "How was that?"

"It was okay."

"Not great?" He handed her a take-out container with a few remaining pieces of a sushi roll. "Spicy tuna."

"Yum, thanks. We went out to play pool."

"Really." He was smirking. "I seem to remember you telling him pretty pointedly last October that pool was not on your list of things you like to do."

"That was then." She picked up a piece of sushi. "I'm open to more experiences now. I'm glad I went."

Zac put a container of cubed papaya on the blanket between them. "You seeing him again?"

A big bite of really wonderful spicy tuna roll gave her the chance to think before she answered. On the one hand, her dating life wasn't really any of his business. On the other, it was a perfectly normal question. If a woman had asked her, she wouldn't have blinked.

But Zac was definitely not a woman. "I thought we were catching each other up on our evenings and the past few months."

"Fair enough."

"So what have you been up to the past few months?" She grabbed another piece of tuna roll. Sheer heaven.

"Let's see." He relaxed down onto his side, supporting his head on his palm. "Before I left, I finished my master's thesis, defended it and passed."

"Hey, congratulations." Chris was taken aback. Before he left? He hadn't mentioned it to her. You'd think he would have been bursting with the news. "What was your thesis about?"

"Introducing clean water systems in isolated areas. I can go into a *whole* lot of detail if you want. It'd take, oh, say, about an hour. Minimum."

"Maybe another time?"

He grinned and stole a piece of papaya. "Then I finished my doctorate program applications and was about to schedule a vacation to Costa Rica when I got the call that Luke had been arrested. He'd gotten into a fight with a kid from another school over something really important, like whose hockey team was tougher."

Chris winced. "Boys."

"Yeah, but I don't cut him any slack for that. He's twenty-one—he knows better than to be a hothead idiot. Plus he'd been on a drinking binge. So stupid. So that took a while to sort out. We all agreed he needed a break from UConn, where he wasn't doing that well anyway, and a break from his usual life, and a break from my dad, who means well but isn't cut out to parent a lost kid."

Chris nodded sympathetically, feeling strangely lit up. She didn't think Zac had ever said that many sentences to her at once, and she was pretty sure he'd never shared that much about his life before. Maybe she hadn't given him the opportunity? "That's a lot to cope with."

"Nah. He's family. He got a bad deal growing up.

My mom died when he was really young. Pretty much a baby."

"Oh, my God, I'm sorry. That must have been devastating." Chris pressed her lips together, aching inside. A bad deal, he'd called it? Typical Zac understatement, undoubtedly representing a hell of a lot of pain, and not only Luke's.

"So Luke is here now. As soon as he finds a job, I hope he'll settle, maybe go back to school at some point if he can get in anywhere around here. But he needs to do some growing up first."

"He's still pretty young."

Zac didn't respond, which surprised her until it hit her that if his mom died when he was a teenager, he'd undoubtedly had to grow up a lot quicker than Luke.

Her heart started a slow sympathy melt.

No. She was not going to allow herself to get soft on Zac. It was really late at night—or really early in the morning—and she was exhausted and therefore a little giddy and vulnerable, and he was an undeniably large, warm, sexy presence beside her in the cool air on the deserted beach, spilling out his heart in a way he never had before.

Breathe in, breathe out.

"Now tell me how *your* last few months have been."

"Oh." She speared another of the sweet, juicy papaya pieces, wishing the fruit was this fresh and flavorful back east. "I've had a really great time."

"Guys been asking you out every hour on the hour?"

"No! That was really weird." She laughed, feeling herself blush in the darkness. "Most of the time I was feeling my way through changes at Slow Pour."

"I like what you did. You got rid of some of the clutter without sacrificing the comfort or quirky feel of the place."

"Thanks." She was surprised he'd noticed, though given how well he could read her feelings, she probably shouldn't be. That was so different from the men she knew. Her father could probably pick up on a hint of sadness if one of the three women in his family was writhing and sobbing on the floor at his feet, but other than that... "And I took a few weeks of classes at the Peace, Love and Joy Center, trying to unblock myself, surrender to a deeper consciousness, and become freer and less stressed."

"Ah."

She frowned. "Are you making fun of me?"

"Me?" He sat up to unwrap a bar of chocolate and broke off a row. "Why would I do that?"

"Because you think I'm spouting New Age crap."

"No." He handed her the squares of chocolate. "I think the idea that you have to fix something about you is crap."

"I'm not trying to fix anything—I'm uncovering the real me. You must think it's possible to change or you wouldn't have brought Luke here."

"Luke is trying to change his perspective and his circumstances. Not who he is."

Chris bristled. "I'm not even sure who I am. The real me has been blocked my whole life, and I'm only just getting at her. You can't claim to know her and what she needs better than I do."

"No, of course not."

Chris struggled to relax. Darn it, Zac had gotten to her *again*. "All I know is that I have felt charged up and mildly panicked my whole life, and now I feel I can be free of that. How can that be wrong?"

"It's not. I'm sorry, Chris. I didn't mean to be disrespectful. If this program is making life better for you, that's a good thing."

Chris waited, a piece of chocolate held so close to her mouth that her salivary glands activated. Was he really as sincere as he sounded, or was he making fun of her again?

He seemed calm.

Yeah, big surprise.

She ate the chocolate, feeling oddly cheated by his surrender, which was crazy. The last thing she needed was more arguing.

"Okay, so now we've discussed our evenings and what we've done for the past few months." Zac shifted on the blanket. "I get to ask. Are you going to see Gus again? Are you going to have dinner with Bodie?"

Chris frowned. "Why do you want to know?"

"Jeez, Chris." Zac exhaled impatiently. "Why do you *think*?"

Another one of those pesky thrills chased around her body. Was he saying he was interested? Jealous, maybe? Stop. At the center she'd identified this crazy-making habit of projecting her own thoughts onto other people and had sworn to avoid it, even if it meant putting herself in awkward or potentially vulnerable situations. From now on, communication had to be honest and clean, always. "Why don't you tell me?"

"Okay, I will." He wrapped his arms around his knees. "Because Gus is interested only in surfing and himself and Bodie is interested only in surfing and himself, plus getting laid as often as possible. Gus will treat you like crap because he doesn't know any better, and Bodie will treat you like crap because at heart he's a misogynist."

Chris straightened, annoyed by his response. He sounded like a big brother trying to keep his naive little sister from dating the school bad boy. "I'm not planning to marry either of them."

"Good." Her response clearly annoyed him, too. "You'll get along fine, then."

Chris retreated into silence, totally aggravated by the tension that had ruined the mood of their evening. And aggravated that she was aggravated because she'd spent so many months deliciously calm. Who cared what Zac thought of her love life? He was—

Stop again. Another old pattern—coming up with an outraged defense to distract herself from the truth. Truth always needed admitting and facing, no matter how hard.

Okay. Truth time. Zac's big-brother answer to her charged question had pricked her ego. Deep down she'd wanted him to say he was jealous of her dating other men. Because…

Because…

Because she was attracted to him.

The minute she admitted the truth, she felt the aggravation draining away, giving her a moment of relief before it was replaced by the almost worse panic of vulnerability.

Why hadn't he stayed in Connecticut?

Okay. He'd asked his hard question, now she got to ask hers. "It's my turn. Do you ever get upset? Behave badly? Go nuts over something?"

"Nah." He sent her a grin. "I'm pretty even-keeled. Not a talent—I was born that way."

"Yeah, not me."

"No kidding." His smile and the offer of more excellent chocolate took any insult out of the words.

"You wait." She let the dark richness spread over her tongue. "By the time I go back to New York I'll be just like you."

"I hope not."

She wrinkled her forehead. "Why?"

"Because I'm not gay."

"What?" Then what he meant hit her and she broke out in giggles. "That was terrible."

"Yeah?" He got to his feet, towering over her in the darkness. "C'mon, I'll walk you home."

She scrambled to her feet. "No, no, you don't need to do that."

"Yes. I do." He stared down at her, hands on his hips. "I need to make sure you get home safely."

What could she say to that? She helped him pack up the picnic things and insisted on carrying the blanket.

They walked back to Eva's house in comfortable silence. Then what had been a friendly stroll suddenly turned into what seemed like the awkward end of a first date.

Breathe, Chris. It's only awkward in your head. Be in the moment.

"Thanks for walking with me." She handed him the blanket, wishing it was broad daylight so she wouldn't have to speak in such an intimate whisper. The stillness around them made her feel as if they were the only two people left in the world.

"You're welcome. I hope…" He stood looking down at her. Chris started to take a defensive step back, then made herself stay put and listen to whatever else he was about to say without judgment or dread, trying to calm her hyper pulse. "I hope we can do this again."

Her immediate panicked response was to say *absolutely not*. Because otherwise, well, something bad might happen.

Like…

Sigh. She'd take the middle road.

"You want to do what again?" She sent him a sly look. "Meet by chance on the beach at one in the morning?"

"Exactly, yes."

"It could happen." Chris forced a laugh, relieved that he hadn't pressed further, and then, all of a sudden, she felt…disappointed.

Argh! How was she supposed to follow her true inner voice if the little brat kept changing its mind?

Okay, truth time—she was disappointed. But as she'd realized earlier, it was late and dark and the air was cool and soft and smelled ocean wonderful. They were both tired, and having opened up to each other a little down on the beach, they'd created the prime conditions for feelings that might not hold up. Yes, Chris had promised herself to live in the moment, but that didn't include doing something she knew she'd regret the next day.

"Good night, Zac." Her voice came out husky and low in spite of her having made an effort to pitch it up high and hearty.

"Good night, Chris."

Thank goodness he turned to go. Because being this close to the enticing outline of his solid masculine body, those feelings that might not hold up were becoming pretty strong. What's more, they had apparently rooted her to the spot, because she stayed put, watching him walk away, feeling hollow and wistful.

Lord. This battle with herself was ridiculous. She knew what she needed to do: get back into the house right now and put him out of her mind.

Zac stopped. He placed the blanket and the cooler on the ground, stood absolutely still for a breath-holding second, then turned back abruptly and she was busted, caught staring hungrily after him. Luckily it was too dark for him to see her hunger, but he didn't need X-ray glasses to notice she hadn't moved.

He started walking purposefully back toward her.

She panicked. "What are you doing?"

"What do you think?"

"No." She put up a hand, warding him off, backing away, not even bothering to tune in to her inner voice. This was fight-or-flight time. "No, you—"

There were few things in the world sexier than being grabbed close for a kiss by a man you desperately wanted to kiss you. As soon as his mouth touched hers, she could do nothing but admit that to herself. Because it was screamingly obvious, even if the feeling only lasted for tonight, that Zac was the most desirable man in the universe and she wanted him with every fiber of her being.

Then the hottest kiss of her life was over. He pulled back and they were left staring at each other with, she suspected, identical stunned expressions on their faces.

Then his hand shot out and pulled off her ball cap. Her hair tumbled down in a wavy mess around her face.

She couldn't speak, couldn't breathe. No wig. No faking now.

"I thought so. Now I'll really go. Good night, Chris."

"Good night, Zac. Thanks for a lovely chat and for the delicious food."

That was what her brain wanted to say. Polite, in control and friendly, as if she barely noticed he'd kissed her. As if kissing like that was all in a day's work for a pair of good buddies. As if his taking off her hat to release her natural hair hadn't felt as if he was undressing her.

But all that came out her mouth, on a long, heartfelt sigh, was, "Mmm."

Zac picked up his gear and continued down the street. He didn't glance back, but she didn't need to see his face to know he was wearing an infuriatingly smug smile.

4

BODIE UNZIPPED HIS wet suit and picked up his board, aware that women on the beach were checking him out. He didn't blame them. It was a beautiful, unusually warm February day, and he was a beautiful man.

He swerved to pass a couple of babes, flexing his pecs for maximum definition.

Damn. They were talking to each other and barely spared him a glance!

He should head to Slow Pour later this afternoon, right before the store closed. That Chris chick looked at him as if he was chocolate. He could probably get some from her. He really needed to get laid.

GUS UNZIPPED HIS wet suit and picked up his board, aware that women on the beach were checking him out, which never failed to amaze him since he'd grown up a skinny dork. But hey, he'd worked hard; he deserved to flaunt his Greek-god physique now.

Behold, most excellent ladies. He strode past them, puffing up his chest.

Damn. They didn't seem impressed. Oh, well.

He should head to Slow Pour for some Suja Juice and

to talk to Chris later this afternoon, around closing time. He knew after their date playing pool that she was totally out of his league. Hell, he'd known that as soon as he first saw her last fall. But a guy could still dream.

ZAC UNZIPPED HIS wet suit and picked up his board. He didn't surf often, but the rush usually cleared his head, and after last night it sure as hell needed clearing.

"Yum." A woman called out admiringly from the blanket she shared with her friend as he walked past.

Zac nodded, wanting to roll his eyes. Yeah, she'd say the same about a rib-eye steak.

He should head to Slow Pour later this afternoon for an espresso and to talk to Chris. He was anxious to see her reaction when she saw him today. Last night, that kiss… Man. They'd definitely gotten to a new place, but if his mess of a head was any indication, he wasn't sure what that place was, or if he wanted to be there. Or if Chris did. Seeing her today might help straighten him out where the ocean, sunshine and breezes had failed.

"HAVE A GREAT AFTERNOON, Chris. I'll see you tomorrow." Summer hugged her temporary boss, curious as to what had happened to her the previous evening. Yesterday she'd been her new weirdly blank self, but when she came in for her afternoon shift today, she was sparking energy—except when she caught herself, which was about every five minutes. Then she'd hold still, breathe in, breathe out, relax her shoulders and get on with what she was doing until she forgot and got nutsy again. It would be funny, except people in distress weren't generally amusing. And watching someone try to fight who she was…that was just weird.

Whatever Chris was going through, Summer hoped

she found peace. Maybe with Zac. If Summer had to give up that dream to anyone, Chris was her first choice. Zac and Eva had been perfect for each other, except there was no sizzle between them.

Outside the wonderful coffee-smelling interior of Slow Pour the air was chilly, though the sun had burned off the morning fog. Summer had walked the three miles to work. Her roommate had borrowed her car last night and hadn't been back by the time Summer had to leave in the morning. So annoying, especially since once Summer realized Janine wasn't back, she'd had to rush crazily through her morning routine so she'd have time to walk to Slow Pour in the early morning fog.

Now that the sun was out, she was actually looking forward to the walk home, and she set out at a brisk pace, gleefully imagining all the housework she'd demand Janine do in penance for not returning the car. Maybe she could finally get her roommate to clear her unread magazines off the coffee table and pick up the discarded clothes in her room.

"I said, 'Hey.'"

Summer yelped and whirled around to find Luke hanging out the driver's-side window of Zac's blue Prius. Those hybrids were so quiet she hadn't heard him pull up next to her with Tori Amos streaming through her earbuds.

"Jeez, Luke." She put a hand to her hammering heart. "You scared me."

"Sorry." He checked the road behind him for cars, then swung those amazing blue eyes back at her, sun glinting off his eyebrow piercing. "You need a ride somewhere?"

She shook her head automatically, heart still beating too fast. "I'm fine."

"Do you *want* a ride somewhere?"

Summer pointed ahead of her, annoyed by her immediate negative reaction. She'd come a long way toward shedding her girlhood shyness, but it still hijacked her when she wasn't prepared. Besides which, Luke set off her internal alarm bell. "I'm going home."

"And...?"

A brief laugh. He'd called her on her indecision. "And so you don't need to drive me."

"But do you *want* me to drive you?"

She rolled her eyes. "Luke..."

"Oh, I see." A corner of his mouth twitched. "You don't want me to know where you live."

He was messing with her. Probably flirting, which made her feel sort of pumped up and giddy. When guys who came into Slow Pour started flirting or poured on too much charm, she turned off automatically. But something about this guy made it bearable. Fun, even.

A car came up the road. Luke pulled onto the shoulder and got out, slamming the door behind him, grinning that cocky, infectious grin as he crossed the street toward her.

She sighed, heart speeding again, willing her mouth not to smile back at him, wondering how much he'd really cleaned up his life and attitude. Her last boyfriend had turned out to be a meth dealer. It had taken her three months to catch on. Her boyfriend before that had been arrested for shoplifting electronic equipment from a big-box store. In both cases she'd had the good sense to get out immediately, but what she needed was the good sense not to get into relationships with troubled guys in the first place.

"I just dropped Zac off at Slow Pour. He wants me to pick him up in a couple of hours. Want to hang out? We could drive up the coast, we could go into San Luis Obispo, we could stay here and talk..."

"On the side of the road?"

"It's a sweet spot." He chuckled, the way Zac did when acknowledging a joke. "Seriously, want to take advantage of this sweet set of geek wheels and go somewhere?"

Summer looked down at the pavement, unable to make up her mind. It wasn't as if she had important things to do this afternoon. She'd been planning to make brownies to go with studying for her child-development class. Maybe clean a little. But both those things could wait, and this guy seemed to need a friend.

Maybe she did, too. She hadn't done anything spontaneous or fun in a while. Not since the night she and Chris got their tattoos. "Okay."

"Excellent." He gestured toward the car. "I've had no one but Zac for company for the past week."

"Could be worse." She crossed back toward the Prius. Luke seemed a lot taller up close than he'd seemed across the counter at Slow Pour, just over six feet, maybe, while Zac was six-three or six-four. "Your brother is a great guy."

"He's done a lot for me." He walked with her around the car and opened the passenger door, an old-fashioned gesture that surprised her. "Sometimes I think I'll never be able to repay him. Other times I want him to leave me the hell alone so I can make my own way."

She waited for him to climb into the driver's seat, again struck by how open Luke was with his thoughts and feelings, even to a virtual stranger. Very different from Zac, who seemed to keep his emotions close. "Weren't you making your own way when you got arrested?"

"Oh. Well, yeah." He put the car in gear and moved onto the road. "There's that."

"You have a temper?"

"Apparently."

"With women?"

"Oh, no." He turned to look at her. "Never like that."

"The road?" She pointed toward an upcoming curve. "Might want to keep an eye on it?"

"Oh, the *road*, right. I forgot." He winked at her, that goofy boyish grin combining with his blue eyes and dark lashes to make him irresistible. She'd bet he could have his pick of women.

The thought strengthened her determination not to succumb. Guys like that—handsome, charming and very aware of it—took it for granted that women would fall for them. She didn't want to be just another number.

"Where do you want to go?"

She thought for a minute and lit on an improbable destination. "In another half mile or so, turn left onto Old Creek Road."

"Where are we going?"

"You'll see."

"Whoa, a woman of mystery." He chuckled, sounding so much like Zac again that she found herself turning to look at him, as if he might have somehow switched places with his brother.

They drove Oak Creek Road through green-brown hills dotted with occasional clusters of low trees.

"So, do you have a boyfriend?"

Summer choked back a surprised laugh. "You don't hold back, do you."

"Why should I? I want to know. If you're dating a guy with a gun and a jealous streak, I'm letting you out at the next corner. If you're dating a jerk with an attitude, I'll sock him in the nose."

"Because that worked so well for you last time."

"If—" His laughter interrupted. "If you're dating a geek who wears plaid shorts, I'll talk you out of him."

"And if I'm single?" She flashed him a curious glance, wondering how he'd handle that one.

"If you're single, the men around here are idiots."

"Thank you." She was flattered even if it was probably just a line. "I'm single, taking a break from relationships."

"Yeah? They haven't been working out?"

"Nope."

"How come?"

She shot him an incredulous look. "No boundaries with you, huh?"

"You want some, you just have to tell me."

She thought that one over for a while. His honesty was refreshing, and in stark contrast to her habit of revealing as little as possible about herself. The less people knew, the less they could judge and find fault. "The last two guys I dated both had serious issues."

"Psychological?"

"Chemical. And with the law."

"Yeah?" He glanced over at her. "So you like guys who are trouble?

"Let's say I'm trying to quit."

He laughed at that. "Yeah, me, too."

She let a few more miles go by, not wanting to sound too eager to ask her next question. He seemed comfortable with the silence. She liked that, too. "What about you? Are you single?"

"Single as the day my girlfriend left me." He spoke with a lilting twang, as if he was singing a country song, and shot her a mischievous grin that took her breath away.

Summer would have to work hard on this not-succumbing thing.

Outside San Miguel, she directed him off Highway 101

and to Mission San Miguel Arcangel, a beautiful church complex dating from the late-eighteenth century.

Admittedly, the destination was a test. She was curious enough about Luke to want to know how he'd react to a decidedly low-tech, low-excitement, highly educational and culturally significant site.

He parked the car and gazed at the tile-roofed buildings and chapel. "You're taking me to church?"

"It's a beautiful place." She opened her door. "The monks made wine here. You can pretend it's a frat house."

"Sweet."

They toured the living quarters of the friars, the kitchen, the peaceful quadrangle and the beautiful church, still with its original frescoes. Summer watched Luke to see if he'd act bored and restless, if he'd crack jokes and focus on himself.

He didn't. He lowered his voice, responding to the hushed, sacred atmosphere, and abandoned his swagger, adapting to the reverent spirit of the place. Luke did let loose one crack that made it plain he'd never become a monk, but that was funny, if not totally obvious.

So he was Zac's brother after all, with depth, gentleness and intellectual curiosity. It fit in with her personal theory that while pain could alter behavior, it couldn't change the core of a person.

The only downside was that Summer's nice, easy reason to dismiss Luke out of hand had been seriously weakened, which made her attraction to him more complicated, and more compelling.

After the tour, they walked back to the car, shoulders and hands bumping occasionally.

"Do you want to go get something to eat?"

Summer glanced at her watch. "Don't you have to get the car back to Zac?"

"Oh." He scratched his head, grimacing. "Yeah. I guess I do."

Yeah, she guessed he did, too, and was grateful for the reality check. Maybe he'd just lost track of time, but she'd bet he'd put that responsibility completely out of his mind, and that it was how he usually operated, doing what he wanted when he wanted, without thought to any-one or anything else—a hot button for Summer, who already felt responsible for herself and her younger sib-lings and sometimes her parents. She wanted to be with someone who'd share in that responsibility, not add to it.

"I'll drive you home, then."

"Thanks." She got into the car and buckled up, feel-ing confused and crabby.

"You trust me enough to tell me your address now?"

"Yeah." She sent him a look. "You do anything that pisses me off, Zac will kick your ass."

He turned on the radio, making a face when a jazz station came on. "I might kick *his* ass for having such bad taste in music."

"Why, what do you like?"

"Guess." He shot her a bet-you-never-will look, all mischief and humor, and pulled back onto the highway, heading south.

"Hmm, let me see." She went through a mental cata-log of her brother's heavy, loud music. "NOFX? Rancid? Judas Priest? Hüsker Dü?"

"Hoosker who?" He shook his head. "Never heard of them. I like more mainstream stuff than that. Linkin Park, Green Day, Panic! at the Disco, Fall Out Boy. What about you?"

"My Chemical Romance, Rise Against, Boys Like Girls. But I also like classic oldies. The Beatles, Motown, and some artists and bands my parents listened to—Joni Mitchell, Crosby, Stills, Nash & Young."

"No kidding." He sent her an admiring glance. She felt as if she'd passed some kind of test and was annoyed at herself for being pleased. "So what's your home life like?"

Immediately she felt herself shutting down. He'd mentioned boundaries—this was one of hers. "It's fine."

"You live with your parents?"

"Nope. I moved out."

"When was that?"

"Right after I graduated high school." She tried to figure out how to change the subject. "I'm nineteen, in case you wanted to know."

"I did. Why'd you leave? Bad stuff happening at home?"

Summer looked down at her hands clasped in her lap. She didn't want to talk about her family. A brief summary of guys she'd dated was one thing. But this was too personal, too intimate. It was stuff she'd only share with someone she felt strongly about. Not because her home life had been dramatic or crippling, just everyday drab and ugly and embarrassing. "Not terrible, not the greatest."

"Don't want to talk about it?"

"Not really."

"Okay." He didn't seem at all offended. "So what's the big life plan from here?"

She groaned silently, not sure what to say. It was a perfectly normal get-to-know-you question, but no one knew about her plan to go to college, and she liked it that way. Zac had caught her studying at Carmia Park one day and she'd been tempted to tell him what she was up to, but he'd let the encounter pass without comment.

That same temptation was dogging her now, but she'd be a fool to trust her secret to a guy she barely knew. Who knew how he'd react? It was hard enough for her to believe her dreams would come true sometimes, and that was without anyone else pissing on them.

"I'm just going to hang at Slow Pour until something better comes along. Maybe get married someday."

"Really?" He turned to look at her, frowning. "No college?"

She fidgeted in her seat, uncomfortable lying, reassuring herself this was none of his business unless they grew close enough that she felt comfortable sharing.

"Nah. It's not for me right now." When he made no comment, she glanced over at him a few times. No reaction? He bought it? She wasn't sure if she was relieved or hurt. "What about you?"

"I'm going to steal cars. No, actually carjack them. And do crack. And meth. And die young in a blaze of stupidity."

"Oh, *that's* nice." She rolled her eyes.

"No, it's not nice. It's crap, like your answer." He glanced at her, looking annoyed. "Hang at Slow Pour? Get married? What are you afraid I'll do if you tell me the truth, suck out your soul or something?"

She whipped around to face him, stunned by his outburst. What the hell was that? "Is this your famous temper?"

"You're a terrible liar, for one thing. And you're studying. Psychology or something. Zac told me."

She couldn't handle the accusing stare anymore and sat back furiously in her seat, folding her arms across her chest. She was utterly pissed off, both at him and at herself for lying when her instinct had told her to confide in him. "I *told* you I was staying at Slow Pour for a while, which is true, and that college isn't for me right now, which is also true. I don't owe you any explanation beyond that."

"Oh, that's nice. Now who has a temper?"

"Back off, Luke."

"Okay, okay, I'm sorry. Don't knife me or anything. I don't need any more trouble."

His humor took her anger down a notch. "I'll try not to."

They drove for a long while in strained silence. Summer felt sick, aware that she wasn't blameless for the change in the mood between them, and that she was being stubborn and immature by not making an overture to peace.

But so was he.

By the time they got to Carmia, however, she was sick of the tension, thinking of the fun they'd had at the mission, not wanting to thwart what could turn into a good friendship that might help them both. "Look, Luke. I'm sorry if it hurt you, but honestly, there are things I don't share with people I don't trust, and that was—"

"Why did you go anywhere with me if you don't trust me?"

Her anger flared again, sharp and hot. Fine. If he was going to keep being a jerk, she'd do the same. "I felt sorry for you."

"Oh, that's great. Thanks. Appreciate it." They were silent except for her terse directions until he pulled up in front of her house. "See ya around."

Summer didn't move. She couldn't let it end like this. "Luke. You're being unreasonable. We only just met."

"I don't date women who feel sorry for me."

She rolled her eyes and shoved open the door. "You said this wasn't a date."

"Get the hell out of my car, Summer."

"I'm gone." She shut the door hard and peered in the window. "Nice temper, by the way. You'll go far with that."

He put the car in gear and shot it forward. Summer watched until he was out of sight, lips jammed together, arms folded over her chest.

Loser. Dork. Psycho.

At least this time she'd gotten out long before she could get in too deep.

5

OH, COME *ON*. Zac stared in disbelief as Bodie pushed through the door of Slow Pour and headed straight for Chris—who was back to wearing that dumb wig again— Bodie's eerily white-toothed grin on full display. It was nearly closing time, and Zac had been about to stroll over and suggest he and Chris go out for a drink. Seeing her today, watching her face light up when he walked in, then immediately shut down into that weird new way she had of not letting herself show any emotion, had just affirmed what he had to do. His next step was clear.

In their last exchange of emails, Eva had hinted that Ames was on the verge of being offered a job at Great Grapes Wine Distributors—an immediate opening. Which would mean she'd come back to California, and Chris would return to New York. After that…well, it was possible Zac would get into Columbia, in Manhattan, but he couldn't figure that into any plans until it happened. If Chris left town in her current skittish state of mind, that would be that—he'd have no hope. There was no point trying to start an intense relationship with a woman who was fighting her feelings that hard.

So he'd left the office, bringing work on drought man-

agement he could do at Slow Pour, intending to propose to Chris that they maintain a casual relationship,
one that involved a whole lot of good-night kisses like
they'd shared last night, and whatever else those kisses
led to—he had a whole lot of ideas on that front. The
arrangement would be less than totally satisfying given
Zac's inexplicably deep feelings, but if he let any hint of
those feelings slip too soon, Chris would have nothing
to do with him.

A decent plan. But now here, once again, was bone-
head Bodie, with Slow Pour about to close and Luke due
back any minute to pick Zac up. Sometimes Zac wondered if this woman was worth all the headaches.

The memory of her warm, instantly responsive mouth
provided the answer.

But man, life was so much easier when it involved only
work and fun and friendship. So simple, neat and tidy—
the way engineers like him preferred things to be. Once
romance and emotions got involved, the world became
a complicated mess.

"Dude!"

Zac looked over in disbelief at the flurry of high-
fiving and fist-bumping.

Gus, decked out in bright yellow board shorts and a
Hawaiian shirt, his dark hair recently gelled, probably
here to ask Chris out again, too.

This was freaking nuts.

He got only a small amount of satisfaction from seeing Chris roll her eyes at the alpha display. Maybe she'd
take his advice and steer clear of both of them.

"Hey! Guys!" She snapped her fingers to get their
attention. "I'm about to close, do you want anything?"

In a movieworthy display of maleness, Bodie took off

his sunglasses and leaned across the counter. "Just the chance to spend some time with you."

Zac held his breath. If she did what any sane woman would do and threw up immediately, there was hope.

She didn't. She lifted a dark eyebrow. "What were you thinking?"

"Aw, man." Gus threw up his hands and let them drop. "*I* was going to ask her out."

"Too late, Barney." Bodie poked him in the chest.

That was it. Zac thumped his laptop closed and stood.

"Zac, dude!" Gus came over for a high five. "Haven't seen you catching any waves for a while. They were cranking this morning on dawn patrol."

"I was out later."

"Yeah? You doing anything tonight, man?"

"Meeting my brother." Who was now apparently going to be his date for the evening. Zac glanced pointedly at his watch, trying not to sound as annoyed and disappointed as he felt. "He's on his way. I'm going outside to wait for him."

He left the shop, giving Chris a brief nod. That was it. He was outta there. She could have her Gus and Bodie and eat them, too.

Twenty minutes later, he was still waiting and utterly pissed off. Luke wasn't answering his phone. Zac could either walk the five miles home, or stand here like a moron, waiting for his loser brother, while any minute Chris would walk by, headed for a date with a mistake in evolution who happened to look like every woman's surfer-dude fantasy.

Not much of a choice.

He headed south on La Playa, aware he was behaving like a cranky child, and not caring. Over the years he'd prided himself on maintaining an easy-come, easy-go mentality about whether any given relationship developed or not. Why fret over a romance if it wasn't meant to be?

Practical, sensible, downright smart.

And then there was Chris. Why couldn't he just say, "Guess she's not that into me," and move on?

Because of the way she kissed you last night.

So? Kissing was a pleasant activity—maybe she just enjoyed doing it. Maybe the power of their kisses hadn't meant as much to her. Maybe it had scared her. Anything was possible. Bottom line: Chris had chosen Bodie, and Zac was done.

A car approached, going too fast. Better not be Luke speeding. The kid had enough bad news on his record.

The vehicle slowed down as it approached him. Great. It was Luke. Zac swung around, putting on a severe frown so Luke would know he was disappointed.

Instead of his bright blue Prius sedan, he encountered a bright red Corvette convertible, top down in spite of the cool weather, and inside, ta-da: Bodie and Chris.

Hadn't he seen this scene in about a dozen high school movies? Hunky hero and sexiest girl in town pull up in latest-model car next to big loser, who is walking down the dusty street because his irresponsible pain-in-the-ass brother couldn't get his act together?

"Need a ride, dude?" Bodie called out, one arm draped along the back of Chris's seat.

Zac sent him a withering look. "Your car only seats two people."

"Oh, yeah."

Zac wasn't going to look at Chris. He didn't want to see her smug and happy in the cool car with the hot dude.

He looked at her, anyway—she was made of some magnetic material his eyes couldn't resist.

She wasn't looking smug. In fact, she appeared to be embarrassed and miserable.

His heart leaped.

Jeez, Zac, calm the hell down. If Chris wanted him, she wouldn't be in the convertible with Bodie. She'd be with him. Walking. On the road. Because Luke was an irresponsible—

"Sorry about that, dude. Well, see ya later." Bodie floored the gas and the car shot away, tires squealing.

Zac would really like to think that Bodie acted the way he did and drove that kind of car because his dick was the size of a dehydrated slug.

Another car came up from behind him and this one also slowed. Zac swung around again, his frown even darker. His brother was in serious trouble now.

But, again, it wasn't Luke. Gus this time.

This day was turning out to be more and more special every second.

"Dude." Gus pulled up mournfully next to Zac, who acknowledged him with a nod, but kept walking. Gus's car—an orange Kia with a cracked windshield—nosed closer and crawled alongside him. "Don't know about you, but after that odious debacle, I could totally use a beer or two, or like three. You up for hitting the A-Frame?"

"I'm heading home, thanks, Gus. Gotta find Luke."

"Is he driving your car?" Zac nodded and Gus pointed over his shoulder with his thumb. "Dude, he's at Slow Pour. I just passed him."

Zac stopped walking. *Great. Terrific. Fabulous.* "Okay. Thanks."

"No problem." Gus drove off, turning his head to shout, "Change your mind about the beers, let me know."

"Sure, Gus." Zac started back on La Playa. Predictably, a text came through on his phone from Luke.

I'm here, where are you?

> Forty-five minutes late. No apology.
> He texted back: Walking home.

I'll pick you up.

A minute later, Luke pulled up beside him. He got into the passenger seat, telling himself not to yell at his brother until he heard his side. But it was tempting, especially because there was a really fine-quality yell building in his chest. But the reasons behind that yell had more to do with his own issues than Luke. Besides which, yelling first and asking questions later was how their dad handled Luke, and clearly that hadn't done much good.

As soon as Zac's door closed, Luke accelerated, cutting off a car coming up the street behind him.

Zac nearly bit his tongue in half holding back fury. "So, how come you were late?"

"Don't start, okay? Just don't."

Zac rolled his eyes. "I'm not *starting*, Luke, I'm just *asking*."

Silence.

Too bad there wasn't an eject button under Luke's seat, though it would probably be a bad idea to get rid of the driver when the car was going nearly fifty miles an hour.

"Sorry." Luke blew out a breath. "Summer and I went to San Miguel."

"Summer?" Zac couldn't hide his surprise. Summer was about the last person he'd picture his brother with. She was sweet and wholesome and West Coast, while Luke was…none of the above. "Whose idea was that?"

"Hers."

Another surprise. If Luke messed with her, Zac would—

Okay, wait, one step at a time. "So what happened? You lost track of time?"

"The date ended badly."

Zac's stomach sank in dread and he clenched his fists. "How badly?"

"It was like the conversation just took a dive. You know? You start out great, and then suddenly you're swirling down a toilet and you have no idea how to back up or get out of it."

Zac snorted, his anger cooling into sympathy at Luke's bewilderment. Yeah, he knew about that. "You like her?"

Luke shrugged, trying to look nonchalant, but his face was slowly turning pink. "She's okay."

"She's great, actually. If you do anything to—"

"I'm *not* going to do anything to her."

"Okay." Zac made himself back off. Another thing their dad did far too often—expect the worst of Luke. "So what are you going to do?"

"I don't know." He slowed the car to a reasonable speed. "What would you do? And don't say, 'Nothing.' That's your wimp style, not mine."

The question was so unexpected Zac had to keep himself from asking Luke to repeat it. He'd even overlook the wimp comment. Mr. Know-It-All was asking his too-rigid, too-serious brother for advice? This was a first.

"I'd apologize."

"I didn't *do* anything." Luke grimaced. "Well, I did lose my temper, but man, she gave it right back to me."

"Apologize, anyway."

"For what?"

"For fighting, for accusing, for existing, whatever it takes. You let a misunderstanding stand like that, and it weighs on you. Especially with someone who could be a good friend, like Summer."

"That is completely messed up. Why should I— Hey, isn't that Bodie and Chris going into the A-Frame?" Luke pointed, and then glanced at Zac, who felt as if someone had punched him in the stomach all over again. "That sucks, huh?"

"Not a good night for the Arnette brothers."

"I thought you guys did okay last night."

"We did." Zac shook his head with exaggerated weariness. "Women, huh?"

"Women!" Luke smacked the steering wheel, grinning. "But you know what you need to do, right?"

Zac was walking right into a trap. "What?"

"Apologize to her."

"Why?" The word came out on a chuckle as he did his best impression of his brother in full outrage. "I didn't *do* anything."

"Dude." Luke started laughing, too, deepening his voice to match Zac's. "Apologize, anyway. For existing. For not being a massive prick like Bodie! You let that shit stand and it *weighs* on you, man. Especially with someone you are completely wussy in love with like Chris."

"Aw." Zac reached over to tousle his brother's hair, as he'd done when Luke was much younger. "You are just so *adorable*."

"Dude! Do not touch the perfect strands." Luke was giggling like his old self, free and unself-conscious. "We are discussing serious business here. We must make a pact to apologize to our completely unreasonable women who hold our balls in their hot little hands."

Zac cracked up. He'd forgotten how funny his brother could be. And in this case, wise. Zac wasn't going to give up on Chris—of course he wasn't. She couldn't possibly enjoy her date with Bodie any more than she had her date with Gus. In fact, odds were she'd enjoy it a lot less. Zac kissing her last night had probably freaked her out and she was having a beer with Bodie in a twisted attempt to protect herself. If Zac stayed patient, his plan could still work. And he might as well practice what he preached and be a better role model for Luke. "Yeah, okay. I'll apologize if you will."

"Deal." Luke picked up speed, then took a right turn toward the Carmia Pier, which was lined with bars, restaurants and surf shops. "But we're going to a different bar first. I'm gonna need a beer or two for courage."

"So IT WAS cranking out there, really firing. I drop in and I'm charging this wave, totally owning the pocket. I carve my bottom turn totally perfect, I'm totally amped, getting ready to kick out, and some goat boater crosses me and I have to bail before I eat it." Bodie laughed bitterly, shaking his head. "Man, that pissed me off."

Chris took a gulp of her third margarita, dimly aware that she was drinking too much too fast, but she had to numb the pain somehow. There had to be a finite number of waves in Bodie's life, and there had to be a limit to the number of details he remembered about each one, right? Please?

"So then, there was this time on Indian Beach when I—"

"Bodie." The third margarita had given her enough courage to call it a night. "This has been great, but I think I'm ready to go."

His face brightened. Chris could have kicked herself. Maybe he'd been boring himself, too? She should have suggested they end their date an hour and two margaritas ago. She shouldn't even have agreed to come—that had been clear about two seconds after she'd said yes. But that morning she'd woken up in a horrendous old-Chris state of anxiety over the kiss with Zac and what it meant and what it didn't mean, and then he'd walked into Slow Pour and she'd wanted him to stay and she'd wanted him to leave, so by the time Bodie asked her out, she'd just wanted something in life to be *simple*.

Bodie was nothing if not simple.

"Awesome." Bodie signaled the waitress. "Where do you want to go? My place?"

Chris blinked. "Uh, I meant I want to go home."

"Okay, that's cool, too." He dug out his wallet. "This is on me, by the way."

"Thank you." Generally she'd insist on paying her half, but after what Bodie had put her through, his paying was pure justice.

"No problem." He shook back his hair, which wasn't really long enough to shake, plus it had been overbaked by sun and dried crispy by salt, so it barely moved. "Money is not a problem for me."

"That's nice." She smiled politely, glad for him. After all, considering his intelligence and personality were clearly lacking, he might as well be rich.

Thankfully the waitress brought back his receipt quickly and they were out of the restaurant and over to Bodie's car in a flash. He drove ridiculously fast all the way to her house, obviously as eager as she was to get the evening over with. And to his credit, he was gentlemanly enough to walk her to her front door, where she leaned in for a quick sisterly hug before she—

Urgh. The hug was not quick. She was crushed against him, and then backed up against the door, where he covered her mouth with his. His tongue seemed to be everywhere, exploring her molars with great curiosity.

Ew.

She broke free. "Um, Bodie—"

"I know, babe, I'm feeling it, too." He leaned in for more, mouth open terrifyingly wide. "Let's go inside and finish what we started."

"Bodie!" She was having a hard time not laughing. "That isn't what... I'm not—"

"Baby. You 'n' me, we could have something as epic as *Lord of the Rings*, as wild as wolves in the woods, as kinky as..." He was clearly struggling. "Kinky as..."

"Boots?" she offered helpfully.

"Yeah, okay, if you're into that, I'm there." His breath was warm on her face. Unfortunately, he'd had something for dinner with a lot of garlic. "All I know is...with what I feel for you, we could set the very ocean on fire."

A snort escaped her. Then another one. No, no, no, she couldn't laugh, she couldn't— She did.

"Has there been a recent oil spill?" Another gale of laughter, then she saw that Bodie was not amused and reined herself in, though one last snort escaped her. "Sorry."

"Hey, so I misspoke myself." He took a step back, looking annoyed. "No need to get all name-calling like that."

Had she called him any names? "Sorry, Bodie, that was uncalled-for. But I'm not interested in spending the night with you."

She might as well have slapped him across the face. He was that stunned. "You're kidding, right?"

"No. No, I'm not. I enjoyed..." She searched frantically for a way to tell him the truth. "I enjoyed the dinner and margaritas, but I'm calling it a night."

"Okay, but we can sleep together another time, right?"

"No." She laid a hand on his cheek. "You are totally sexy, but you're not the guy for me."

"Damn. I thought I was in." He rubbed his shoulder thoughtfully. "It's Zac, huh. You like smart guys."

Her eyes shot wide. "What? No. He's— No. Zac's just a friend."

"Whatever." He shrugged. "Well, okay, guess I'll go back to the bar and try again."

Chris blinked at him. Did he really just say that? "Gosh, Bodie. You sure know how to make a girl feel special."

"Yeah." He grinned and gave her a thumbs-up, already backing down her front walk. "That's what they all tell me. See ya around."

He swaggered back to his convertible. Chris went into the house, closed the door and stood for a few seconds, trying to comprehend a universe that would produce a specimen like that.

Eva would love this. She grabbed her cell phone and dialed her sister.

"Chris, oh, wow." Eva burst into nervous giggles. "I can't believe you just called me."

Chris frowned. "Why?"

"Oh, because—" Ames's voice rumbled in the background. "Right, okay. I don't know, Chris. I was just thinking about you!"

Chris was mystified. What was Eva up to? Had she been swimming in the margarita bowl, too? "We're twins, Eva. This happens all the time."

"I know, but…" The line became muffled. Eva's and Ames's voices mumbled urgently.

"Eva?" Chris wandered into the living room. "What's going on?"

"Nothing. Nothing, sorry, I was distracted. So how are all your hot California men doing?"

"Funny you should ask." Chris told her the Bodie story, sparing nary a detail. By the time she finished, Eva was giggling madly.

"Oh, Bodie. So hot, and also *so* not. But I'm glad you're done with him and Gus, because that means Zac is next on the list."

"Zac's not even *on* the list." She sounded so knee-jerk panicked even to herself, that it was obvious Zac was not only definitely on the list, but sitting right at the top in bold, all caps, underlined twice.

Damn it. She should not have had more than one drink tonight.

"Oh, right, Chris, right. Zac's not on the list. Yeah, okay, I believe you."

Chris's heart started beating wildly. She could not even *think* about Zac without anxiety clouding her vision. In fact, she was getting all worked up and annoyed right now. "He and I had a late-night talk on the beach yesterday."

"Ooh, yes?"

"It was okay at first, and then we had a disagreement. I'm telling you, we just don't get along. So then he walked me home." She was getting more and more worked up, pacing Eva's living room. "And then, when I said good night, he *kissed* me."

Eva gasped. "Wow! This is—"

"I couldn't *believe* it!"

"Oh. You couldn't?" Eva sounded confused. "Why not?"

"Well, I mean—" Chris gestured to the air, trying to remember why this had seemed like such an outrageous story when she started it. "I mean, we weren't on a date or anything. It was like…so wrong! And so—"

"Chris?"

Her arm dropped. The classes she'd taken at the Peace, Love and Joy Center had made her question why she flew off the handle like this, but her alcohol-fogged brain was not working well tonight, so…forget it. "What?"

"Men kiss women they like and are attracted to. This is what happens here on our planet."

Chris wrinkled her nose. "I *know* that."

"So…? Was it a good kiss?"

The best ever. "Yeah, it was okay. But that's not the—"

"Ha! You are such a bad liar. I don't even know why you are *trying*. Especially with me!"

"Right. I know." She sank into a chair, feeling suddenly hopeless. "It's stupid."

"What is? What's going on? Are you falling for him?"

Chris took in a deep breath, let it out, eyes closed, except the room started swimming and she had to open her eyes to steady it.

"No, of course not." Her voice cracked. "I just can't seem to help wanting him like crazy."

"Aw, Chris. I know it's scary. When I realized how I felt about Ames, I totally freaked out. Commitment-phobia to the extreme."

"But I've had long-term relationships before. I've never felt like this." She sounded whiny and pathetic.

"Chris." Eva was breathless with excitement. "Maybe he's *The One*."

"No. No, he is not The One." She was certain of that. "We totally get on each other's nerves. He's maybe The Eight or The Nine."

"Why don't you just have a fling with him, then?" Eva's voice had turned sly. "You said that's what you wanted to do while you were out here—I mean out *there*. At least Zac isn't an idiot like Gus and Bodie."

Chris blinked. Blinked again. A glow of excitement started in her chest. Her heart slowed and she felt a huge weight lift. That could actually work. As long as she wasn't falling for him, which, when she was sober, she'd need to figure out for sure. Her inner self was happy with the fling idea. Look how quickly her panic and confusion had dissipated.

However. Chris was *not* letting her sister know she was even considering the idea. Eva would start planning her and Zac's wedding before they even got to climax together.

Ooh. Nice thought. The climax, not the wedding.

"Eva, I don't think that's a good idea."

"Why not?"

"Because…because…" Inspiration hit. "Zac isn't the fling type."

Eva snorted. "He's a guy. All you have to do is say some variation of, 'Hey, wanna do it?' and he's yours. Men are very simple creatures."

A vision rose of Chris saying that to Zac. Of his face darkening with desire, his arms reaching for her, his body backing hers into her bedroom, down onto her bed and—

A sound broke into her daydream. Huh? What was—Oh, right.

"I have to go. Doorbell's ringing!"

"Ooh! Go see who it is. If it's Bodie or Gus, do *not* let them in. If it's Zac—"

"Ha." Chris snorted on her way to check. "It's not going to be Zac."

"It could be."

"You should have seen how he looked when he saw

me with Bodie. Like he wanted to rip me out of the car and feed me to bison."

"Bison are herbivores. Who is it?"

Chris checked the peephole and gasped, clapped her hand over her mouth. "Oh, it's Bodie. Holding my sunglasses. I must have left them in his car. Talk to you later, Eva, bye."

"Don't let him in!"

"No, no, don't worry. Bye!"

Chris hung up the phone and stood motionless, collecting herself, feeling guilty for rushing her sister off the phone, and also feeling unbelievably fizzy. Then she grabbed the handle and swung open the door.

To Zac.

6

CHRIS TOOK A moment to center herself before she spoke, only it didn't work at all, and she ended up giggling instead. She'd just decided she wanted to sleep with this man, and here he was! Carmia was an amazing place. And she'd turned into a giddy mess.

"Hello, Zac." She'd tried to sound in control and deeply at peace, but instead she sounded formal and ridiculous. She might as well have said, *Good evening, Zachariah.* That made her giggle again.

"Chris?" He looked concerned.

"No." She put a finger to her lips and looked around cautiously before she whispered, "I'm Angelina Jolie. Tell no one."

"Are you okay?"

"Extremely. Why?"

"Nothing. Are you alone?"

She was filled with excitement at the question, thinking he might be about to propose the very same fling she wanted, until she realized he wasn't necessarily interested in being alone with her, he could just be asking if she'd brought Bodie back to the house tonight. "Yes! I'm alone. Did you think I brought Bodie home with me?"

"The thought crossed my mind."

"Then why are you here?" She narrowed her eyes suspiciously. "Were you hoping to watch?"

Zac looked surprised for a split second before he snorted. "I think I'd better come in."

"What for?" It wasn't exactly a polite question. She wished the tequila would magically exit her brain. "Well, I mean, are you going to kiss me again? Because I'm not sure that's a good idea when I've had a couple of margaritas or three."

His brow rose. "Only if you want me to, Chris."

Yes.

"Hmm." She backed up and tripped over whatever was behind her that was trippable.

His strong hands caught her—not that she was going to fall—but it was good to know his reflexes were excellent in case she needed him to catch bullets or something.

The thought made her giggle again. "You can come in."

"Thanks." He walked over the threshold, making Eva's tiny house seem even tinier. "I take it you had a good time with Bodie tonight?"

"You know what?" She closed the door behind him. "You are so sweet to be so relentlessly and none-of-your-businessly concerned about my dates with other men."

"Yeah, I'm precious." In the soft light she could see the tension in his face, which was otherwise irresistibly handsome. "How did it go?"

"It was fabulous. Amazing. The best night of my life." She gestured dramatically, gazing off into the distance as if remembering fondly. "We dined on oysters and filet mignon, sipped champagne and thousand-year-old brandy and discussed politics and philosophy and literature and music."

Zac's eyes narrowed. He folded his arms over his chest, which made him look even larger and more stern, and which made her want to giggle and jump him all at the same time. Funny how he'd annoyed her at first and then got sexier and sexier, while Bodie had made her weak with lust at first sight, then turned distinctly icky. "Did he behave?"

"Pretty much." Chris brought her arms down. "Nothing I couldn't handle."

His body tensed. "What does that mean?"

"Zac, Zac, Zac." She sighed with exaggerated exasperation. "He wanted to sleep with me, but I didn't want to sleep with him and told him to go away and he did. Okay?"

"Okay." Zac relaxed visibly. "Good."

Chris rolled her eyes. "Can I have my allowance now, Dad?"

He glared at her. "If he had done anything worse than annoy you, I would have gone over to his house, taken his surfboard and shoved it—"

"Ew, yes, okay. Please do not go on." She held up a hand to stop him, secretly thrilled at his knight-in-shining-armor protectiveness. "Don't need to hear those details."

His glare didn't ease. "Are you seeing him again?"

"Didn't I say that was none of your business?" She jammed her hands on her hips and glared right back. "No, of course not. You and my sister were both right. He's creepy."

As if she had super fairy-dust magic, his glare cleared. "Smart girl."

"Me or Eva?"

"Yes."

"Thank you." She walked over toward the kitchen,

feeling euphorically light and free, but also in control of her emotions and the situation—the perfect balance. However, she had decided very sensibly that she shouldn't proposition Zac while her brain was still ruled by El Jimador Blanco, since life decisions made in that condition were not exactly trustworthy. "So, do you want a drink or anything? I'm going to have about a gallon of water."

"I'll have water, too. I'm not staying long."

She was disappointed. And also not. Being around Zac tonight, broad and solid in a blue polo shirt that brought out the intense color of his eyes... Well, in her margarita-induced state of weakness, it would be too easy to give in to lust and invite every bit of the inappropriate behavior she hadn't wanted from Bodie. Too soon to make that call.

Maybe first thing in the morning.

"Come, sit." Holding their water glasses in hand, she led him into her sister's living room, eclectic and colorful, just like Eva. A drab beige couch was enlivened by a Mexican shawl, richly colored pottery brightened every surface, and a black-and-teal-painted table drew focus to the center of the room. Eva was the type of person who could buy something ridiculous, throw it somewhere and have it instantly make a chic and fabulous statement.

Maybe Chris just tried too hard. Her New York apartment was efficiently furnished and color coordinated. When she got back she'd do something to make it more playful. Like install a full-size photo of Zac on the ceiling over her bed.

She handed him his water and waited for him to sit, then realized he was being a gentleman and waiting for her.

Hmm. If she chose the couch, he might sit next to her,

and she'd be in danger of falling victim to the warmth of his large and deliciously muscular body.

Yum.

If she chose a chair, he would have no way of sitting next to her and she'd be in no danger of falling victim to the warmth of his large and deliciously muscular body.

Darn.

She dodged the issue entirely by staying upright.

As did he.

"Well." She sounded ridiculously chipper, the way she always did when she was nervous. It was going to be very hard to keep to her temporary vow of chastity if Zac made the slightest move. Like if he blinked. "Was there any reason you came by tonight besides making sure I wasn't conceiving a bunch of mini Bodies?"

"Actually, I came over to apologize."

She stared up at him. "Apologize? For what?"

"I have no idea." Zac downed a gulp of water. "I was hoping you'd know."

"Me?" She was officially baffled. "What do you mean? Am I angry at you?"

"Hey, I remember this." He picked up an exquisitely detailed redwood carving of a sea turtle from the bookshelf. "I gave this to Eva when she first moved to Carmia. What was that, five years ago? Three? I've lost track."

Chris could cheerfully slug him. Did he know he was reducing her to utter confusion yet again? Did he do this on purpose?

"What am I being apologized to for?" She frowned, wondering if that held up grammatically.

"Luke and I had a talk. We agreed it's a good idea to apologize to women."

Chris snorted. "That is sexist and ridiculous."

"Is it?" He tossed the turtle from one hand to the other. "I'm sorry."

"Apology accepted." She moved closer on the pretense of examining the little turtle. "I remember Eva telling me about this and about you. She was sort of in love with you back then."

"I was sort of in love with her, too."

"But you never did anything about it."

"Nope." He put the carving back on the shelf and stared at it, his back to her.

"Why not?"

"I'm not Bodie?"

"Oh, *whew*. That is such a relief. I thought—"

"Some people you can love and still be satisfied with friendship." He turned. "Others not so much."

Chris took in a breath that seemed to go on forever. How was it possible to have that deep an effect on a person with just words and a look? She felt as if she was slowly drowning, except this water was exceptionally warm and clear and sweet and inviting. Even her wise inner voice was waving pom-poms and chanting, *dive, dive, dive*!

Or maybe that was just her hormones. She wasn't going to listen to them. They'd been drinking.

But Zac seemed to be talking about something a hell of a lot more intense than a fling if he'd mentioned the L-word. That was not her plan at all.

"Zac, I'm sorry. I don't want to get seriously involved with you."

His eyebrow quirked. "Did I just ask you to?"

"Oh. Um. No." Her face grew red. "No, but, well, you kissed me last night, and then tonight you showed up, and just now you said that about friendship and love and now

I'm exactly the crazed babbling character I don't want to be, and it's all because of you."

"Maybe that's what I was apologizing for."

"I don't know." She sat on the couch, plunked her elbows on her knees and her chin in her hands, stomach churning acid. "I just know I can't think straight when you're around."

"Yeah?" He sat next to her, folding his hands between his long thighs. "That makes two of us."

"Really?" She lifted her head, feeling a little more hopeful. Idiocy apparently loved company. "What should we do?"

"I was thinking we should be friends." He put the glass to his mouth and mumbled something very peculiar.

She was sure she hadn't heard him right. "Wind buffets?"

"Uh. No." He put the glass back down. "I said, 'with benefits.'"

Chris sat there stupidly for two seconds until a fluttery little dance started in her chest. But…this was exactly what she wanted. She and Zac were on the same page for probably the first time in their entire friendship.

Still, hadn't she decided she wouldn't have a fling with him until she was sober? Her chest tightened. Her stomach went back to sick. Yes, she had. "Zac, I…think I need time to process that one."

"Understood." He leaned in so his shoulder pressed against hers. Even that innocent a touch was sexy when it was Zac. When Bodie had squashed her against the front door, she'd felt a whole lot of nothing. "Unless we're both sure that's what we want, we shouldn't agree to anything."

Chris nodded, relieved at how sweet and understanding he was being, and miserably disappointed because she was ridiculously hot for him and wanted his body immediately.

There wasn't a single other person in her life who managed to elicit opposing reactions in her time after time. She turned toward him and found herself staring at his beautiful mouth. "That sounds very sensible."

Sensible.

God, she was heartily sick of sensible. Her entire focus of the past two months had been on trying to escape the evil clutches of sensibleness. Look how she felt now that she'd decided to ignore her pom-pom–brandishing inner voice and keep from jumping Zac's delicious bones tonight because it was more *sensible* to wait. Sick! Tense! Miserable! How much more proof did she need?

"It does sound sensible, doesn't it." Now he was staring at her mouth, which was practically buzzing with the need for him to kiss her. "So…I better go before I do something I won't regret."

She giggled. "You think you wouldn't?"

"I know I wouldn't."

Eva's clock ticked off a whole bunch of seconds. A breeze fluttered the curtains.

"Chris." He leaned in a couple of inches closer.

"Mmm?"

"I'm not moving away from you, am I?"

"Let me check." She pretended to inspect, moving closer herself. "Hmm, nope."

"I don't think I can. So it's up to you to move away if you want. Because I'm going to kiss you."

"Oh, my." Chris stared at his spectacular mouth. She could practically taste it again. "That sounds like a terrible idea."

"It gets worse." He leaned toward her until his amazing lips were mere centimeters away, and his warm, non-garlicky breath was brushing her skin, turning her slowly molten. "Because if I kiss you, I'm not going to want to stop there."

"Oh! That *is* worse. *Much* worse." She was imagining his hands on her naked body, his warm torso lowering over hers. Or under hers. Or behind hers. Or—

His mouth tasted just as wonderful as it had the other night, and the pressure of his lips ignited a fierce and primal response in her, just as it had the other night.

But unlike the other night, they were on a nice soft couch, and unlike the other night, her defenses were somewhere down around her ankles. Chris wanted this. She'd invited this. She didn't need defenses.

He pushed her back on the couch—or had she moved there herself, inviting him along? She didn't know. But the passion that came to life between them, her legs locking around his, their hips straining toward each other, that was definitely mutual.

Also unlike the other night was the…the…

She struggled under the haze of passion to recognize what it was she was hearing.

The doorbell! Again!

Zac's eyebrows flew up, then immediately crashed down. "Expecting someone?"

"No." She held his eyes, breathless, not wanting him to move off her. "No one."

The bell rang again, followed by aggressive knocking. A man's voice.

Zac got up and headed toward the door, body tense, face grim.

Uh-oh. Chris followed him anxiously. If either Bodie or Gus were outside, she felt really, really sorry for them, and *really* hoped that whoever it was, he hadn't brought his surfboard.

It wasn't either Bodie or Gus.

"Eva!" Chris stood stock-still before throwing herself into her twin's arms. For the first time in her entire life she was wishing her sister wasn't on her doorstep. Or on Eva's own doorstep. Or whatever. "I was just talking to you! Why didn't you tell me you were already here?"

"I wanted to surprise you."

"You did, you did!" Chris laughed drily. *Yeah, no kidding.*

"Zac!" Eva sent Chris an oh-my-God-you-owe-me-details look before giving him one of her passionate embraces. She looked her wonderful kooky self, with her bright red-framed glasses and a green knit cap over her blond hair, peacock earrings that dangled to her shoulders and a polka-dot top over scarlet leggings tucked into black ankle boots. Strangely, for once Chris didn't feel drab and boring next to her. Maybe the tequila…

"Hi, Ames." Chris hugged him hard. Funny how when Ames had been pursuing her in New York, Chris had found him cold and soulless. Now standing next to her sister, he was instantly likable, handsome even, with warm brown eyes Chris immediately trusted. What an amazing transformation. "It's great to see you."

"Same here." He turned to Zac. "I'm Ames Cooke, nice to meet you, Zac."

The two men shook hands.

"So, what are you doing here?" Chris poked her sister in the arm, resigned to no hope of returning to make-out heaven. "Who is minding my store?"

"Jinx is in charge, just for two days. Ames passed all the phone interviews at Great Grapes with flying colors so he's here to meet the bigwigs for the in-person rounds." Eva was on fire with energy and love for Ames. It was wonderful to see.

But her message was somewhat less wonderful to hear.

If Ames was hired, he and Eva would be moving back to Carmia. And if they were moving back to Carmia, that meant Chris would be moving back to New York.

And if Chris was moving back to New York, that would mean her time with Zac, newly redefined and opened up to a whole new world of possibilities, would be even shorter than they thought.

7

BODIE SAT MOODILY at the bar, back at the A-Frame, trying to figure out what had gone wrong. Chris had been so hot for him she could fry an egg on the sidewalk. He was sure. She'd done that same squirmy, pink-cheeked blush thing all chicks did when he gave them his Sex Look.

Damn.

Maybe she was playing hard to get. Maybe he should have been more persistent, though she'd sure sounded as though she meant no when she said it. But if he went back tonight and—

"Hey, is this seat taken?" A blonde took the empty stool next to him without waiting for his answer, flipping her hair and smiling seductively, her breasts prominently displayed in a low-cut, clingy top.

Whoa.

Okay, never mind about Chris. He was good.

ZAC DROVE TOWARD his house, faster than he needed to be going. It had been so great to see Eva. So great to meet Ames.

But had they *had* to show up just *then*? His guy parts

were still furious. *Hey! What happened? We were almost there! You can't do this to us!*

He'd finally been able to put Bodie and Gus safely away, and this woman who had haunted him for the better part of the past five months would finally belong to him…in a truly tentative and messed-up way.

Yeah, okay, that last part sucked. But he couldn't tell Chris the extent of his feelings. She could barely handle the lying version. It was all part of his master plan: if the relationship felt disposable, Chris wouldn't feel so anxious. Then, under the astounding spell of his irresistible charm, she'd be free to discover or develop feelings for him.

Of course, the plan could backfire. He could fall even deeper and she could bolt from fear, or never feel anything for him. But crossing the country hadn't been enough to get her out of his head. Trying to ignore her here hadn't worked, either. He had to try something else, and, to his great surprise, Luke had been his inspiration, encouraging him never to give up. Yay, team.

Except now, with Eva and Ames back at Eva's place and Luke camped out at his place, there was nowhere private in Carmia short of a motel room in which he and Chris could explore the benefits part of their friendship. If Ames got a job offer in the next few days, he and Eva would be making plans to move back ASAP. Just as he and Chris were finally making progress, they'd end up on opposite sides of the country once again.

He was as pissed off as his parts.

He wondered if Luke had kept his part of the bargain and gone over to apologize to Summer. Maybe he'd be hanging out with her tonight until nice and late? If the house was empty he could text Chris and invite her over.

Or if Luke was asleep, they could creep into Zac's bedroom and...

Nah. He needed a plan B. Maybe they could pitch a tent somewhere? That was scraping the bottom of the idea barrel, but it was a possibility. First, though, he'd cross his fingers that Luke was at Summer's house. With all his clothes on.

Ten minutes later that hope died a quick merciless death. Luke was sprawled on the couch in front of the TV, which was making relentless exploding sounds.

So it was either sneak Chris in or sneak a tent out. He wasn't sure how she'd feel about either, but the way she'd responded to him, and the way her face froze when she saw her sister, he had a feeling she'd wanted this as much as he did, and might settle for less than ideal conditions to make it happen.

"How's it going?" Zac was determined to come across as normal and calm, though he felt as if he was shooting electricity from every nerve. "You apologize to Summer yet?"

"Nah."

"Why not?"

Luke shrugged, not looking away from the TV. "I'll do it tomorrow."

"Dude, you chickened out."

"No, honest. I thought it over and decided I'd give her more time to cool down, bring her breakfast tomorrow morning or something. She was seriously pissed. Why, did you apologize to Chris?"

"Yeah." He tried not to look smug, but he was probably not very successful. Luckily Luke's eyeballs were frozen to the set. "It went well."

Understatement of the year. Though if Eva hadn't shown up, it would have gone even better.

"Good. I'll try it tomorrow. Maybe she won't kill me."

"That's all we can ask." He gave a fake yawn. "So, um, I might be going back out in a while."

"Yeah?" Luke smirked, still not turning away from the set. "Oh, wait, you can't."

Ha! Try and stop me. "Why not?"

"That chick came by. Jackie. She's asleep in my room. Said you should wake her when you got in. And by the way, you were totally right." He nodded solemnly, eyes wide. "In-*cen*-diary."

No way. No freaking way. *Tonight?* "She said she was coming Saturday. That's tomorrow."

"She came a day early. Said if it was a problem she could crash at a hotel. I said it was cool." He finally managed to tear his eyes from the TV to peer curiously at his brother. "Why, are you going back out with Chris?"

"Who's Chris?" Jackie emerged from the guest bedroom, dark hair rumpled, big eyes sleepy, her clingy T-shirt ending midthigh, nipples poking out from the thin pink fabric.

Luke's eyes popped out of their sockets. Zac didn't blame his brother. Jackie was unfairly hot. She was also incredibly smart and dedicated and sweet—unless you got on her bad side. Then watch out.

"Hey, Jackie." He strode over and gave her a hug, gathering her tight, smelling her familiar smell, incredibly glad to see her and also wishing she was anywhere else. "It's great to see you."

"You, too, Zac. Who's Chris?" She gave him a look he knew well: dark eyes narrowed, one eyebrow up. The look of a police interrogator.

"A woman. A friend."

"He's *totally* hot for her." Luke's tongue was still hanging out—figuratively, thank goodness. He'd better not get any ideas. Jackie would eat him for lunch.

"Hmm." Jackie's hands went to her hips. "And you're supposed to meet her tonight?"

"Well, I thought maybe. You know, just to hang out. Talk. For a while. On the beach."

"Just talk?" Again the interrogator look.

"Yeah, talk." He had a feeling he wasn't convincing her. "We're friends."

"Well, then, why not invite her here?" Her voice was uncharacteristically high and musical. "I'd *love* to meet her."

"Oh." He tried to fake enthusiasm, he really did. "Well, yeah, I could do that."

Jackie smacked him on the shoulder and burst out laughing. "I was kidding. I showed up a day early. You shouldn't have to cancel any plans because of me."

"Okay."

Oops. He probably should have waited at least a couple of seconds before jumping on her offer. Though at this point, he and Chris would be reduced to the tent idea. It was a really nice tent, but...

"So tell me about her." Jackie shook her long hair to one side and tipped her head to look up at him. "How long have you been dating?"

"I know exactly how long."

"Aw, how sweet." She looked vaguely ill.

Zac pretended to count. "No months, no days and no hours."

"Oh, so this is totally new?" Jackie put her hands on her hips, stern again. "Does she know how you feel about her?"

"Of course not," Luke chimed in. "If I hadn't yelled at

him, he'd still be sitting there sucking his thumb, waiting for her to show up with a box of condoms."

Jackie burst into her great deep belly laugh. "I can totally picture that."

Zac knew looks couldn't kill, but he gave it a good try, anyway. They both deserved the effort. The short version was that Jackie had practically had to drag his emotions out of him when they'd started dating.

"Go." Jackie made shooing motions. "Go have fun with your 'friend.' I'll watch TV and get to know your gorgeous brother."

"Cool." Luke moved to make room for her on the couch, looking half thrilled, half terrified. As he should.

"We'll wait up for you!" Jackie chirped.

"Oh, no." Zac tried not to sound desperate. "I wouldn't do that."

Jackie settled in beside Luke, whose eyes resumed their popping. "Planning to stay out late, are you?"

"Actually, yes. I won't be back until late."

Jackie shrugged, looking way too innocent. "*I* don't mind staying up late. You, Luke?"

"Not at all."

Zac glared at them both. "*Really* late."

"Like I said, not a problem. Luke?" She nudged him with her elbow. "You mind staying up *really* late?"

"Not a bit." Luke smiled sweetly at his brother. "We'll be here waiting for you to see how all that 'talking' went with Chris."

Zac clenched his teeth. "I mean like late morning."

"Well, Zachary." Jackie folded her arms over her chest, face in a familiar deadpan. "I myself am shocked. Luke? How about you?"

Luke gave him a thumbs-up. "I'm *definitely* apologizing to Summer first thing in the morning."

"Luke, this isn't about—"

"I know, I was *kidding*." He looked to Jackie for approval—or at least to her breasts for approval.

"Does she have a place in Carmia?" Jackie calmly turned Luke's face back toward the TV.

"She's staying at her sister's." He thrust his hand through his hair. "Unfortunately, as of tonight, so is her sister."

"Aw, man, that sucks." Luke kept his eyes fixed on the TV, his face bright red from Jackie's intervention.

"No problem. Remember the friend's cabin I told you about? Where I'm going next to do my hermit thing? It's empty. You want to use that?"

Zac stared at her. Come on. No sneaking in and out of his bedroom? No tent? Perfect solutions didn't just drop into people's laps like that. "Are you serious? You don't think she'd mind?"

"Of course not, or I wouldn't offer. She told me I could bring friends if I wanted." She jumped off the couch and headed for the guest room. "Hang on, I'll get the directions and keys, and you can be on your merry way."

Zac turned from staring after Jackie to staring at Luke, still trying to figure out how something had finally gone really right today.

If Chris agreed to go with him…very soon they'd be friends getting all the benefits they could handle.

"So? Tell, tell! What was Zac doing here?"

Chris snorted, half tempted to tell her sister exactly what they'd been doing. Maybe she and Ames would be horrified at having intruded and would check themselves in to the Carmia Court Motel for at least one night. Her female bits were aching and wistful, having come so close to satiation—no amount of meditation was going to help relieve this stress.

But she wasn't quite ready to share yet.

"Zac?" She blinked innocently, knowing she probably didn't fool her sister for a second. "He was checking on me after my date with Bodie. Making sure I was okay."

"Oh, right, uh-huh. Making sure you were okay." Eva snorted. "Why, did he have some reason to think you wouldn't be?"

"Well, yes. He thinks Bodie's convinced he has sexual rights to all his dates."

"That wouldn't surprise me. I mean he must score all the time. He is *so* hot, that—" She jumped with a squeak and glared accusingly at Ames. "I was *getting* to the bad parts."

"As long as you remember he has many." Ames kissed her on the cheek. "Thousands, in fact."

"I know. Such a shame." Eva sighed forlornly. "But back to Zac. It's significant that he came to check on you, Chris. That kind of protectiveness means something. Not to mention the chemistry between you guys is hot enough to melt lead. Did you see how he was looking at her, Ames? Aren't they perfect for each other?"

"The only thing I think is that I'd better bring our stuff in from the car." Ames winked at Chris, who grinned back. She liked this new version of Ames. She could even forgive him and Eva for barging in on her and Zac just as things were getting really good between them. Why had she waited so long and wasted so much time on Bodie and Gus? Maybe she'd just needed to get to this new place of self-confidence or whatever it was before, she could—

"—or not?"

Oops.

Eva had just asked her something. "Sorry, what?"

"Ha!" Eva looked triumphant. "You had a totally goopy, dumb look on your face. I knew you weren't listening. It's Zac. It's got to be Zac. Something happened tonight."

"Okay, okay, it's Zac." She flung up her hands and let them drop.

"I knew it!" Eva pumped her fist, sending bracelets jangling down her arm. "This is fantastic. It would be so great if things worked out between you. Or hell, if you got married. Maybe after you move back to New York, you can—"

"*Whoa*, Nelly."

Eva cracked up at Chris's dead-on imitation of their father's dead-on imitation of a character from the old Roy Rogers show. "Sorry, sorry. I just got so excited."

"Nothing is going to 'work out.' We're just hanging out for a while. It's totally low-key. When I go back to New York, he's going to graduate school and that's that. No big romance, no big deal."

Her text signal went off. She dragged her phone out of her pocket.

I'll pick you up in half an hour. Pack a change of clothes, a toothbrush and a flashlight.

Chris gasped. She felt her cheeks turn red. Zac wanted to finish what they started *tonight*, even though Eva had just arrived. The thought made her feel a little giddy and a lot crazy. For once, she didn't mind.

He didn't want to wait.

And in a big, meaningful rush she realized her own truth: neither did she.

"Chris! What is it?"

Chris stared at her sister, mind whirling. Zac couldn't

be inviting her to his house. Luke would be there, which would be awkward, to say the least. They couldn't stay here, either, so where…

Wait, a flashlight?

Camping? Ew.

"Um. It's nothing. Really."

"Uh-huh." Eva folded her arms across her chest and peered at Chris over the rim of her red glasses. "From Zac?"

"Mmm-hmm. From him. Yes."

"Ah. So this is 'no big deal' and 'totally low-key,' which is why your eyes are the size of quarters, fireworks are shooting out the top of your head and you can't come up with more than two-word phrases."

"My eyes are fine." She squinted comically. "And it *is* no big deal. Zac just wants to hang out tonight, probably on the beach or something, just to talk."

"Goody." Eva grinned angelically. "Then Ames and I will come with you."

"Oh…" She would not let her face fall. She could not. It must not.

It did.

"Ha!" Eva pointed triumphantly. "You're busted. I was right. If this isn't a romance, it's sure as hell about to be. From there it's only a matter of time till you fall completely and madly in love with him."

8

As NERVOUS AS she was, it was a relief when Zac's car pulled up in front of the house and Chris could step through the front door, away from Eva's knowing smiles, winks and questions. Sweet of her to want so badly for her sister and her best friend to fall for each other, but this relationship was definitely not going to be about love. As usual, Eva preferred her version of the world to what was right in front of her face, so no amount of explaining and/or protesting from Chris would faze her. It wasn't even worth trying.

Now, with Zac waiting for her, the nerves were taking over, broadcasting excitement, not alarm, so she knew she was doing the right thing. Just as she knew she was doing the right thing by letting her hair fall naturally, displaying only one pair of earrings and wearing leggings and a loose shirt that were, ahem, easy to get out of.

"Hi." She climbed into the passenger side of his Prius, thinking how much she preferred it to Bodie's turbo testosterone.

"Hi." He was smiling that great Zac smile that made her insides turn over. "You look fantastic."

"So do you." He'd changed into a white shirt and jeans,

one of her favorite looks on a guy. Very sexy. But Zac could be wearing plaid overalls and she'd still want him.

He put the car in gear and moved forward. "I feel like a teenager sneaking out of the house to make it with a hot girl in the middle of the night."

"You're not far from it. Where are we going?" Chris tucked her tiny overnight bag at her feet and buckled her seat belt, hoping his answer didn't contain the word *campground*.

"A friend has a friend who has a cabin about half an hour up the coast."

"Sounds great." Ah! Thank God, no camping. Though who knew what kind of place this cabin might be if she needed a flashlight. As long as it had a roof. And a bed. And running water. And flush toilets. And no bugs.

"How are you feeling about this?" Zac turned north onto La Playa. It was strange being in the car with him, chatting casually, driving toward a place in which they'd get naked and sweaty together for the first time.

"Nervous." She gestured between them. "This is nothing I would have done even a couple of months ago."

"No kidding. The drive to Connecticut would have been ridiculous."

She broke into giggles. "I mean with any guy."

"You'd do this with *anyone*?"

"Well, sure, of course. You just asked me first. Well, second. But Bodie was never seriously in the running."

"I'm glad to hear that." He put his hand above her knee and squeezed. She wanted to open her thighs wide and let him explore. Feel his fingers slip under her panties and get to know her intimately.

Mmm. She squeezed her legs tightly together, released them, squeezed again. Somewhere she'd read that women could make themselves come that way.

Lucky.

Parting her thighs a couple of inches, she leaned back, wondering if Zac would get the hint, not sure enough of herself to make it an obvious invitation. She'd never had sex with a guy she knew less about. And never imagined she could do something like this and not be freaking out.

Zac took his hand away. Apparently he didn't get the hint. Maybe it was just as well. She probably would have caused an accident.

"So you've never had a casual relationship like this before?"

"Nope." Chris surreptitiously pulled herself back up in the seat. "I've always been a boyfriend-and-girlfriend dater. What about you?"

"I've been in relationships I knew wouldn't last forever, but not like this."

Chris frowned. For some reason she'd assumed he did this all the time. "Why did you suggest it with me?"

"It seemed to fit us."

"Because you'll be going to graduate school and I'm moving back to New York soon?"

"More or less."

She frowned harder. Strange answer. Especially since Zac was usually very precise. "If you didn't have much time with a woman, but felt seriously about her, would you still want the relationship to stay casual?"

He glanced over, then back at the road. "If I had serious feelings and thought they had any hope of being returned, nothing would keep me from trying for forever."

"Oh." Aanother of those crazy deep-down thrills. The idea of Zac letting nothing stop him from going after a woman… A traitorous part of her wanted to be that woman, to have the experience of meaning so much to someone that he'd sacrifice anything.

Stop. No. Chris needed to live in this moment, not in some theoretical one. Besides, that kind of reckless passion wasn't her style. "Have you ever been that in love?"

He sent her one of his amused looks. "These are some pretty intimate questions."

"I'm getting to know you."

"Yeah? Is that necessary for what we're doing?"

The question shocked her. Was that what he wanted? For the sex to be as anonymous as possible? She'd expect that from Bodie or Gus, but not Zac. "Not necessary, no. But not bad."

He maneuvered around a sharp curve, and she swore he was looking smug. What was with this guy and the smugness?

"To answer your question, I did think I was in love once. A woman I dated for four years after college and before I joined the Peace Corps. But when things turned bad I knew it wasn't the real thing."

"Why, you think love lasts forever?"

"I do."

From anyone else, the naïveté would seem absurd. But in that masculine voice, spoken with deep conviction, the belief carried weight. "What about all the people who get married and then grow apart? You're saying they were never in love?"

"I think you can make a mistake, yes. Infatuation can be so strong and so convincing that people rush into marriage. Most divorcing couples I know have pretty clear hindsight about why they weren't compatible."

"You're a romantic."

"I am." He wasn't apologizing.

"But you're okay with casual sex."

"Casual sex can be very romantic."

She frowned. "I never thought of it that way."

"Really?" He glanced at her. His hand found her thigh again. "I've been thinking of sex with you that way."

"You have?" Chris opened her thighs a bit wider, a smile hovering on her lips. She really liked this new calm Chris. The first time she had sex with her last boyfriend, she'd been giggly and stupid with nerves, half wishing she was curled up alone in a quilt watching TV with a mug of hot cocoa. The Peace, Love and Joy Center was the best thing that had ever happened to her. California was the best thing that had ever happened to her. "Tell me more about that."

Zac's smile widened. Her mind raced ahead. In these fantasies of his was she bent over the arm of his couch? Naked on the beach with her legs spread wide? Straddling him in his bed? Kneeling in front of him with her mouth around his—

"I like thinking of you on the beach, sun lighting your face, laughing, your energy flowing, but relaxed, loose and free. I imagine you not worrying about anything or anyone, even yourself."

Chris turned to stare at him. A sweet, melty ache started in her chest. "That's it?"

"What?" He glanced over at her, back at the road. "You don't like it?"

"No, it's wonderful." Her voice came out throaty and low. "Just not what I expected."

"What did you expect?"

"Oh, something like…me naked and hog-tied."

"Wow." He gave a short burst of laughter. "Actually, I could work with that. But I wouldn't classify that fantasy as romantic."

"I guess not. Honestly, the whole romantic thing isn't that important to me. I'm more concerned with respect and compatibility than grand gestures and passion in a

FREE Merchandise is 'in the Cards' for you!

Dear Reader,

We're giving away FREE MERCHANDISE!

Seriously, we'd like to reward you for reading this novel by giving you **FREE MERCHANDISE** worth over $20. And no purchase is necessary!

You see the Jack of Hearts sticker above? Paste that sticker in the box on the Free Merchandise Voucher inside. Return the Voucher promptly...and we'll send you valuable Free Merchandise!

Thanks again for reading one of our novels—and enjoy your Free Merchandise with our compliments!

Pam Powers

Pam Powers

P.S. Look inside to see what Free Merchandise is **"in the cards"** for you!

◄ Detach card and mail today. No stamp needed. ►

© 2013 HARLEQUIN ENTERPRISES LIMITED ® and ™ are trademarks owned and used by the trademark owner and/or its licensee. Printed in the U.S.A.

FREE MERCHANDISE VOUCHER

2 FREE
BOOKS
and
2 FREE
GIFTS

Please send my Free Merchandise, consisting of
2 Free Books and **2 Free Mystery Gifts**.
I understand that I am under no obligation to buy
anything, as explained on the back of this card.

150/350 HDL GGCF

Please Print

FIRST NAME

LAST NAME

ADDRESS

APT.#   CITY

STATE/PROV.   ZIP/POSTAL CODE

NO PURCHASE NECESSARY!

HB_215_FM13

relationship." Her words hung in the air, pompous and dull. She shifted in the seat, stomach tightening. Was that even true anymore? Had it ever been?

"Chris." His hand landed on her thigh again, voice dripping with sympathy. "I'm so sorry."

Chris giggled, her stomach relaxing again. She pitched her voice to a prissy chirp. "I believe it's only sensible to wait for sex until mutual respect is cemented, a minimum of sixteen years."

"Ha!" He looked at his watch. "How about sixteen minutes?"

"Okay." She spoke in her natural voice again. "Sorry about that flashback to Old Chris. I didn't realize how horrible I was."

"Not horrible. Afraid."

She waved him away. "No, no, not fear, a block."

"Uh-huh. And those are different because…"

"Oh." Chris grimaced. "You're right, those are the same thing. Either way, I've been boring my whole life."

"Trust me, you are not that."

"Not anymore." She opened her thighs wide this time, no mistaking her meaning, and leaned back in the seat, thrusting up her pelvis. "California, here I come."

Zac inhaled sharply. The car swerved. "Holy—"

He brought the Prius back under control, then his hand took the trip she'd been hoping for, lazily stroking her inner thigh, getting closer with each back-and-forth until his pinky brushed against her sex through the thin material of her pants.

Oh. My.

Just that light touch set her whole body on fire. If he did it again she was going to lose control and beg.

He did it again. A firmer touch this time, with an even more powerful effect. Chris let herself feel it all, head lolling against the seat, too overcome with passion to hold it up.

Zac's fingers settled into a regular rhythm. She whispered his name breathlessly, clutching his forearm. He continued rubbing lightly back and forth over her clitoris until she was panting and close to coming.

No, no, this wasn't the time. "You should probably stop now."

"Why?" He didn't.

"Because..." She could barely get the word out. "I'm going to come in the car."

His low chuckle pierced the fog in her brain. "That's kind of the idea."

Chris closed her eyes, blushing in the darkness. "I just meant...I want to come with you later."

"Chris..." He paused his hand. "You can do that, too."

"No, but I mean..." She was about to explain to him that she only came once a session, but two things happened. One, it occurred to her that she might not have had the most thrilling sex partners, since she tended to go for men as cautious and controlled as she was, and two, his fingers started in again, and the arousal that had slowly started to recede came roaring back.

"Let it go, Chris." His voice was low and gentle, as if he felt he had to reassure her that her head would not, in fact, blow out the car roof. "Come for me."

Oh...oh...oh... She flung her arms over her head, pressing back into the seat, letting out a shrill cry that instantly embarrassed her. The orgasm hit hard and fast, sweeping her along on a sharp rush that peaked and hung before it let her down on the other side.

Zac cursed under his breath, swung the car off the road and jammed it into Park. His seat belt flew off. Hers went next.

The next few minutes were an increasingly frantic and comical series of thuds and *ow* and *sorry* and *I can't quite reach* and *no, that won't work, either* until they both burst out laughing, Chris with her pants hanging around one ankle, leg cramping up on the dashboard, Zac draped across the middle of the car, unable to get his long legs out from under the wheel.

He fell back on the seat, breathing hard. "I give up."

Chris gave a last giggle. "Epic fail."

"We'll do better inside." His hands clamped her cheeks, he brought her face close. The kiss was long and lingering, with a touch of sweetness that made her feel a little unsteady, even sitting down.

Zac leaned back, buckled his seat belt and backed up a few feet, before swinging sharply left across the road.

"Are we turning around?"

"Nope." He drove straight toward the coast, headlights revealing a driveway. "Cabin's right here."

"This is it?" She paused from re-dressing to peer out the window. "We were stopped right opposite?"

"You have no idea how hot you looked." His voice was deep and growly. "I couldn't even wait thirty seconds."

"Oh." Chris smiled at his profile and ran a hand through his thick hair, still amazed at how comfortable she felt with him. She wasn't one of those women who could come at the drop of a hat, and here she'd climaxed for the first time with him in a moving car with all her clothes on. "Sorry it didn't work out."

"I should have known I'm too big to have sex in a Prius."

"Yes, you are." *Yum.* She liked that about him.

They bumped along on the rutted dirt road for about a hundred feet until the headlights picked up the glint of windows. Chris's jaw dropped. "That's a *cabin*? I was expecting a tin shack. Maybe logs."

"She said cabin. I'd call that a house." He put the car in Park and hopped out, coming around like a gentleman to help Chris, who was already out, bag slung over her shoulder, clutching her flashlight and gazing up at what looked to her like a villa.

"Wow. That is some place. How many bedrooms do—"

She was suddenly backed up against the car and Zac was kissing her as if he'd been barely holding back the entire drive up, his body large and warm against hers.

"—you think it has?" She was breathless, laughing. She liked Zac's hidden caveman impetuous streak. He'd always seemed so completely controlled.

"There are four bedrooms. I vote we baptize all of them."

Chris tsked. "Think of all that laundry."

Oh, God. Did she really just say that?

"Actually, Chris." He let his hand trail down her cheek. "I'm thinking of a few other things."

"You're right, you're right. It's a lot more than just laundry." Chris grimaced. "Let me get my calendar, because we'll need to schedule a *full* cleanup session after every—"

Her sentence ended in a shriek because she was suddenly hanging over his shoulder, being carried resolutely toward the front door, the glow of his flashlight wavering on the gravel drive.

Her giggles came out as if she were twelve instead of twenty-eight. This was crazy and silly and she *loved it*.

They reached the front of the house, where she was jolted higher onto his shoulder. Then again.

"What are you *doing*? I'd like to keep dinner inside, where it belongs."

"Getting…keys from my…pocket."

She couldn't stop laughing. "You're going to *kill* me!"

"Nah." The door opened and he brought her in, kicked it shut, hesitated, sweeping the beam of the flashlight back and forth, then resolutely marched them…somewhere.

Then she was being lowered to her feet and was not at all surprised to find herself in a bedroom, Zac's light searching around. An amazing and enormous bedroom. Crazy paintings and sculptures covered the walls and surfaces. Contorted, misshapen bodies tangled around each other, and strangely combined animals roamed eerie mountain and woodland settings. The flashlight created wavering shadows that stretched and contracted across the walls and ceiling.

"Wow. Is your friend a collector or an artist? Or both?"

"Friend of a friend, and I have no idea. Not my kind of art, anyway." He struck a match, lit a kerosene lamp next to the king-size bed and replaced the glass chimney. A warm, steady glow lit their side of the large room, a surprising amount of light given the flame's tiny size. But the effect was still, frankly, creepy.

"She doesn't have electricity?"

"Apparently she's an off-the-grid kind of woman."

"Well." Chris looked around, nodding politely. She was still glad they weren't camping, but she wasn't sure she wanted to make love for the first time with Zac in a Grimm's fairy tale, either. She didn't think she'd be able to relax and think sexy thoughts with a half bear, half reptile glaring at her. "It's…interesting."

"I have a better idea." He caught her chin and kissed her. "Do you need to use the bathroom first?"

"Mmm, probably should." She was not sure she'd ever get enough of his mouth.

"We passed one. Out in the hall, first door on the right."

Inside the bathroom, Chris lit a candle and freshened up, grinning at her reflection in the mirror. Her eyes were large, lips pink and full. She looked happy. Happier than she had in a while. She felt more alive, too, and more free, as if she'd stripped off too-tight shapewear. She even really liked her own hair.

The smile turned troubled. Hadn't she spent the past few months thinking she was finally alive and free, having risen above the shackles of routine and self-control? What was this, then? *Jumbo* alive and free? Maybe she was just giddy with anticipation. But something felt profoundly different about this mood.

Shrugging, she finished drying her hands and hung the leopard-print hand towel back on the gold towel rack. This whole self-transformation thing was turning out to be really confusing.

Zac met her in the hallway with his flashlight, the creepy bedroom dark again behind him. "Ready?"

"We're doing it right here?"

He chuckled. She loved that low, deep laugh of his. Though when it was at her expense she still wanted to smack him. "How about we take a look at the beach? My friend said something about shelters out there. We can at least check them out."

"I would love that."

Outside the air was chilly and she was glad for her sweatshirt and even gladder for Zac's warm body next to her and his arm across her shoulders, though the house sat in a protected cove, which kept the breeze and waves gentle. Overhead the sky was crammed with stars, blotted out in large patches where clouds floated overhead. Chris could also see what looked like a couple of small cabins—this time the word was appropriate—between the house and the water. As she and Zac neared, the structures came into better focus and turned out to be…

Oh. My. God.

She turned to Zac at the same time he turned to her. She didn't need the flashlight to know they were both grinning. The cabins weren't cabins at all, but curtained beachside cabanas, wooden posts at four corners, fabric tented over the top, pulled back to reveal the sky to the occupants.

And they had beds. Big ones. Full or queen.

Chris walked around the perimeter to the ocean side, feet sinking into the soft sand, breathing in the salty sea air. "I think I might have to be appallingly rich someday myself."

"Yeah?" He'd crawled onto the bed and was lighting a propane lamp hanging from the ceiling.

"I mean, I think I deserve a mansion with a private cove, don't you?"

"Doesn't everyone?" He offered her a hand to climb up on the bed.

"I suppose." She turned to sit on the edge of the mattress, then let herself fall back. A breeze blew across her, undulating the curtains. The lamp above them turned out to be a heater, which kept the chill from being unpleasant. "Zac, this is incredible."

"Better than the circle-of-hell bedroom back there?" He lay down next to her.

"Much." Inhaling deeply, Chris stretched her arms up toward the sky. "Look at the stars."

"Look at the beautiful woman in bed with me," he whispered.

She turned, smiling, to find him gazing at her in a gravely awestruck way that made her smile fade, and a solemn, sweet feeling take its place.

Zac moved first; their lips met, clung, met again. Their bodies drew toward each other, arms encircling, legs tangling. Zac didn't seem in the hurry she'd come to expect from men, tasting every part of her lips—one at a time, both together, then the corners of her mouth.

The effect was a remarkable mixture, drugging her nearly into a trance, while at the same time sparking a low burn of arousal that grew until she was the one ready to take things further.

She rolled Zac onto his back and unbuttoned his shirt, taking her time, kissing the skin that was revealed inch by inch. His chest was smooth and well-muscled, warm and inviting. She lingered over one nipple, bathing it with her tongue, pleased by his soft groan of pleasure.

He half raised his body to help her take off his shirt, then she pushed him back down, feeling strong and free and oddly without self-doubt, as if she'd made love to him before and knew what he liked and how he liked it.

The fly on his jeans she undid next—more buttons where she expected a zipper, but they gave one after another without her having to fumble. Underneath, a bulge covered by smooth gray cotton. Chris pressed her face to the soft material, inhaling his scent, moving her lips across the hard length of his penis, loving the way he held still for her, his hand lightly threaded into her hair, not pushing, not guiding, but letting her explore at her own pace.

Slowly, she worked his jeans down over his strong thick thighs, over his long shins and beach-toughened feet.

"Wait…in the pocket," he whispered. "Condoms."

Chris grinned. She had a bunch stuffed into her pockets, too. At least they'd be well supplied.

She pulled the packets out of his jeans and tucked them under one of the pillows, then returned to her task, dragging his boxer briefs down over his erection, which sprang eagerly free.

His body was beautiful, long, lean and masculine, dominating the bed. She felt strangely moved by the trust she had in him not to abuse his power.

"There's a problem, Chris."

"What is it?" She echoed his whisper, even though they could probably shout and no one would hear them.

"Only one of us is naked."

"Hmm." She kissed the tip of his penis, then took the first inch slowly into her mouth and let it back out. "What do you suggest?"

"Take your clothes off for me."

She took him in between her lips again, farther this time, loving the way he reacted with a sharp breath, his hands making fists against the white sheets but his body keeping still.

After a minute or two of tormenting him with her mouth, she let him go and knelt next to him, drawing her top up and over her head, hoping to torment him in a different way. Under it she wore a lacy black bra that earned a murmur of masculine approval, which encouraged her. She reached behind her to unhook it, and with a start realized she had no worries about the size and shape of her breasts, or whether Zac would find them too small, too pointed, too whatever.

Chris was enjoying this fling so much. No anxiety, no worries about whether she was right for him or he for her, just *here I am, here you are, let's do this.*

The bra slid off. Zac's cock jumped. "Mmm, Chris, you are so hot."

Her confidence grew even more. She slid her knit pants down her hips, sat on the bed to kick them off, then knelt back on the mattress, watching him enjoy the sight of her breasts, then drop his gaze expectantly to her panties.

She let him wait until he looked up questioningly and caught her sly smile.

Mistake.

Growling, he lunged and yanked down her panties, toppled her over and dragged them off, tossing them over his shoulder onto the sand.

Then his hands clamped on her hips and he lowered his face until it hovered between her legs, abruptly silencing her shrieks and giggles.

Oh, my.

The cool breeze blew over her, the waves rolled in, the heater whirred.

At the first touch of his tongue Chris nearly lifted off the bed. The warm, wet strokes were doubly intense after she'd been lying wide-open to the chill of the night air. Taking her cue from him, she relaxed instead of straining her hips to his mouth as her body was begging her to do, allowing him to control the process.

Within minutes she discovered that not moving allowed her to concentrate minutely on the intimate movements of his tongue, on the slippery wetness and the skillfully varying strokes and pressures.

His fingers joined his tongue, spreading her labia, allowing him to travel down and around, painting her fully.

Chris moaned and lifted her head, let it drop, clutching at the sheets, on the verge of going over again. She hadn't thought she'd be able to come twice, now she was barely able to hold back.

"Zac."

"Mmm?"

"Not now. Not yet. I want to come with you inside me."

"You will." He thrust a finger up into her, closing his lips over her clitoris and sucking hard. Chris gave a choked yell and a second orgasm swept her, lifting her to a burning peak for one long, nearly unbearably intense moment before the sensation burst and spread, leaving her convulsing under Zac's mouth, her internal muscles squeezing around his finger.

Eventually, she recovered sufficiently to speak again, between still-fast breaths. "Oh. My. Gosh."

He kissed her clitoris lingeringly, nuzzled the inside of each thigh, then kissed his way up her stomach. "You liked that?"

"Um. Yes?" She laughed, shaking her head in disbelief. "But we have another problem now."

"What's that?" He lay next to her, propped up on his elbow, hand possessively on her stomach, his erection poking her side.

"I'm ahead by two."

His deep chuckle delighted her. "Yeah, I'm pretty pissed off about that."

"I don't blame you." She slid her hand surreptitiously under the pillow, looking for a condom. "It's greedy of me."

He shook his head mournfully. "Pret-ty selfish."

She came up with a packet and held it to his chest, then pushed him over on his back. "Your turn."

"Oh, boy." He was so eager she found herself giggling again. She'd never been able to play like this in bed, to laugh and not take the lovemaking completely seriously. This change was delightful.

Had she mentioned she liked flings?

"Hold still, Zac. This won't hurt a bit." She tore open the packet and rolled the condom onto his erection, which was so hard she had no trouble whatsoever.

He helped her to straddle him, grasping her hips and guiding her over him. "Now?"

"No, no, not yet. First we're going to have a long discussion about—"

"Now." His strong hands pushed downward. His cock found her, pressing strongly, demanding entrance.

She closed her eyes, savoring the hardness between her legs, the promise of joining to him in this incredibly intimate way. "I guess now is okay."

"Mmm, good." He let her weight sink her down, allowing the tip of his cock inside her, stretching her, sending nerve signals firing.

Chris gasped and let out a moan, unable to believe how she could still be this turned on after coming twice tonight. She lifted, then sank again, her arousal increasing. Once more and she was rewarded with the long, slow, easy slide of Zac's erection inside her, and the ragged breath, almost of relief, that told her this felt really, really good to him, too.

She rocked her pelvis back and forth, concentrating on the length of him filling her completely. "Mmm, Zac, that is really nice."

"Yes." He spoke tersely. "*Really* nice."

Smiling, she planted her hands forward on the bed, and lifted and lowered her hips, savoring the slip and slide of him, in and out, in and out.

"Chris." He was breathing with difficulty, hands urging her along as she pumped him.

She opened her eyes to find him watching her, jaw clenched, chin jutting, and pretended concern. "Hey, are you okay? You look sort of…desperate."

"Um. Yeah. You're making me kind of nuts."

"Gee, is that bad?"

"At my age I'm supposed to be able to last all night."

"So I must be doing something wrong?" She lifted up off her hands, balancing her weight over her thighs, and crossed her arms behind her head, arching her back, riding him harder, up and down, up and down…

"No." He was barely able to speak. "Definitely not… Oh, my sweet—"

A breath hissed out between his clenched teeth, his fingers dug into her hips. He gave a brief yell and held her still over him and she felt him pulsing inside her, over and over until he gave a soft groan and lay still.

Pleasure welled up inside her, too. She felt crazy sexy, like nothing she'd ever felt before. Maybe it was the romance of the cabana, the wild isolation of the cove and the distant awesome beauty of the stars. But she suspected it had more to do with the man in this beautiful bed.

"Come down here with me." He pulled her on top of him, wrapping his arms around her.

Chris burrowed against his chest, closing her eyes, inhaling the warm skin under her cheek.

He stroked her gently, her hair, her back, her arms, occasionally dropping kisses on the top of her head.

"Oh, Chris."

At his whisper, in the midst of her satisfied afterglow, lying in his strong arms, an unexpected sweetness stole over her. And an unexpected longing.

Zac started talking, stroking her, telling her how he'd wanted her for so long. Telling her how much he admired what she'd accomplished at the shop, how much he enjoyed her sense of humor, her strength, her spark and fire.

The sweetness spread through her chest, and she thought of how she'd wanted him for so long, too, though her blocked self wouldn't let her recognize it. And how much she admired what he'd accomplished in his life, and how much she enjoyed his sense of humor and his strength...

Then he turned her face up to his, rolled her onto her back, covered her with his large, strong, comforting body and kissed her as if she was the most amazing woman he'd ever come across or would ever come across.

No, no. A fling was all she wanted, all that was good for her, and it was all Zac wanted, too. Any other feelings would only mess that up.

9

GUS OPENED ONE eye blearily to sunshine and blue sky, sand under his cheek. Huh? He lifted his head and blinked, squinting. Aura Beach. What the—?

He moved cautiously into a seated position. *Man*, he was stiff. What had—

Gus let out a groan. Last night, Pete's Tavern. That girl had come on to him. She was sorta hot, not really, something kind of off, but he'd been doing shots and wasn't in a picky mood. They came down here, smoked a few joints—killer stuff—had some laughs, and then things had just started happening...

Aw, man. He buried his head in his hands and crumpled sideways back onto the sand.

Chicks should not turn out to be dudes, that was all he had to say about that.

"Did you have a heart attack?" The child's voice surprised him. "My grandfather had one. Mom said he keeled over. Is that what you just did?"

He lifted his head. Little girl. Blue eyes, blond curls, five or six years old. Totally cute. "Nah. I'm okay."

"Mom says I'm not supposed to talk to strangers, but I thought if you were dead it would be okay."

"Where's your mom now?"

"At home." She pointed carelessly over her shoulder. "Aunt Pammy brought me."

Gus's gaze followed her finger. His jaw dropped.

Hurrying toward them, blue eyes, blond curls and awe-inspiring curves outlined by a wet suit was a woman—a *real* one this time. He was sure.

She was carrying a board.

Gus rose unsteadily to his feet, heart pounding, mouth dry, head buzzing like he was still high.

This was it. She was it.

He was in love for the very first and very last time in his life.

SUMMER WOKE TO a pounding on the door. What time was it? She'd been awake for a while around five, her usual time to get up for work, but had managed to go back to sleep. She peered groggily at the clock next to her futon. Ten! She hadn't slept that late in forever. Ugh, she hated wasting so much of the day.

The pounding sounded again—the downside to a broken doorbell, which the landlord had dragged his feet about fixing. Summer should just give up and look for DIY instructions online, which was what she did for most things that broke in the house. Their landlord had seriously draggy feet.

She grabbed a robe she'd had since early high school, purple flowers on a pale cream background—first thing she bought with her very first paycheck from Von's grocery store—and wrapped it around herself, hurrying toward the door.

"Coming." It was probably her brother, Ted, who always knocked as if he were being chased by zombie cops. "Who is it?"

"Hey! It's me. Open up!"

She started, eyes widening. Not Ted. *Luke.*

Oh, great. After the unpleasantness last time she saw him, she'd get to encounter him again with stinky breath and bedhead, her futon in the living room still open and made as a bed.

Though maybe he deserved it.

She opened the door, not sure what to expect or how to act around him. "What are you doing here?"

"Hey, good morning, beautiful day. Aren't you glad to see me?" Grinning, eyes hidden behind the smoky-gray sunglasses, he held up two take-out bags from Slow Pour. "I brought us breakfast."

At the sight of him all her anger—okay, most of it—melted away, and she was perversely, ridiculously glad to see him. She'd spent way too long going over their argument and had concluded that neither of them deserved medals for good behavior. Though of course Luke had behaved *much* worse than she had. "Why should I be glad to see you?"

"Because I'm here to apologize for being a dork. After you accept, we can be friends again and hang out again today. Let me in?"

Summer made an exasperated sound, barely able to keep her mouth from twitching. His arrogant charm was potent stuff. "You're taking for granted that I'll forgive you?"

"Sure. You will, won't you?"

She sighed and stepped back. "You might as well come in."

"Sweet." He seemed taller in the house, looking around openly with his glasses tipped down. He wasn't wearing the eyebrow ring today. She liked him better without it. "Nice little place."

"It works for us."

"You sleep in the living room?"

"It's a one-bedroom. My roommate sleeps in there." She pointed to Janine's door, kept closed because it was easier than getting her to tidy up.

"She still asleep?"

"She's over at her boyfriend's place. She spends most nights there." Why was she telling him this?

He followed her into the tiny kitchen. "You should get the bedroom if she's not here that much."

"Bedroom occupant pays more rent." Summer opened the door to the refrigerator. "I'm going to shower and dress. Do you want some orange juice?"

"I brought some. Sort of." He put the bags on the counter and pulled out a bottle of Suja, looking bemused. "It's orange, anyway."

"That's their Bliss mix. It's awesome. Suja juices are really good."

"If you say so." He dipped his hand into the bag again. "Though there's one flavor called Master Cleanse. I'm telling you, I do *not* even want to know."

"Welcome to California." She gestured to the stove, where her bright red kettle gleamed like new. If you took care of stuff it didn't need to look as old as it was. "Should I make coffee?"

"I've got that, too. And muffins. I brought a bunch. I didn't know what you like."

He wasn't kidding. He had about six of the huge, delicious muffins they sold at Slow Pour and several different kinds of juice. It must have cost a bundle. She loved the food and drinks served at the shop, but no way could she afford them.

Wait, Luke didn't have a job. Was Zac footing the bill for their breakfast? That wasn't right.

"Who paid for all this?" The second the question was out of her mouth she wanted it back. So not her business.

"I did." He looked annoyed. He had a right to be. "That a problem?"

"I'm sorry, that was rude of me." She felt herself blushing. "I just… I worry about money all the time. But it's not my place to worry about yours."

"No, it's not. But it's *really* not cool to assume I would throw money around I didn't have." He opened one of the coffees and took a sip, watching her over the rim of the cup, eyes challenging. "You don't know me—why expect the worst?"

Summer's stomach turned sick. He was right. She'd adopted a superior attitude from the beginning, as if he was the poor little screwup and she was perfect. She could suddenly see their fight in a different light, and it looked as if she might have been the one who behaved worse. "I'm sorry for that, too."

"If you want to know the truth, I'm a spoiled rich kid. Mom's family has tons and Zac and I inherited. Feel better?"

No, she didn't. "It was stupid to assume—"

"And make an ass out of you and me." He grinned that charming grin. "Go shower and don't worry about it, Summer. Really. I know how I come across. I'm working on it, along with a crap load of other stuff. Soon I'll be without any flaws at all, just like everyone else."

"Aw, Luke…"

"I'm serious. Go clean up. I'm hungry." He gave her a gentle nudge. "Go. It's really okay."

"I'll be back soon." She fled to the bathroom, still feeling awful. Somehow she'd gone from being the injured party to the injurer. Instead of blaming her, Luke had been incredibly understanding and sweet, which made her feel worse. She wasn't used to that. Her family disagreements escalated exponentially and loudly, the emphasis on winning rather than communicating.

But then, Luke hadn't been raised in her family. A rich kid from Connecticut? He might as well have been born on another planet. She wasn't sure why that bothered her so much. Because she no longer had an advantage? God, she hated to think she was that type of person.

There was another possible reason, one she wasn't crazy about acknowledging. Luke had seemed approachable as an irresponsible, drifting screwup. If he was an East Coast prep school trust-fund baby, that put him about as far out of her league as Zac was.

So be it. Summer had managed to be friends with his brother; she could be a friend to Luke, too, tell her heart to stop beating so quickly around him, and focus on her own life and her own goals.

She showered quickly, brushed her teeth and threw on sweatpants and a pink cotton sweater, not bothering with makeup. Luke had already seen her without any and she didn't want to seem to be primping for him.

By the time she got back to the kitchen, he'd found glasses and plates and arranged their breakfast on the table, in the center of which stood a vase containing white tulips and purple hyacinths.

"Luke." Summer clasped her hands to her chest. She couldn't remember the last time a guy had given her flowers. And this guy did so after she'd insulted him. "Where did those come from?"

"The florist."

She rolled her eyes. "I *mean*, where did you hide them?"

"Outside your door." He was clearly pleased with himself. "If you hadn't let me in or weren't home, I was going to leave it. The lady told me the purple ones mean I'm sorry and the tulips stand for new beginnings. I figured that about covered it."

"Thank you." She was deeply touched. Not only had he gotten her flowers, he'd cared about which ones to buy.

"Yeah, well, I'm sorry about the fight after San Miguel." He looked it, too, sincere and a little embarrassed, all his smugness gone. "I was pissed because we had a nice time and I felt like you could be a real friend, and then you said you didn't trust me, which is stupid. Of *me*, I mean, to be pissed that you didn't. I thought we were...I don't know. I'm kind of a mess right now, so I shouldn't blame you."

"I get it. I really do." She folded her arms across her chest. He was being really sweet again. One minute after she'd told herself to keep it under control, her heart was racing again, and she was feeling weirdly vulnerable. "I shouldn't have said I felt sorry for you. That was mean and not really true the way it came out."

"It's okay, you were mad. I like that you give as good as you get." His grin came back halfway. "So...we're good?"

"We're good."

They smiled at each other until the awkwardness was nearly unbearable.

"Okay, we are *so* done with the emotional crap." Luke made a sweeping motion with his hand. "Let's eat and have fun."

They ate muffins and drank coffee and juice, debating options for spending the rest of the morning together, and finally settled on the short drive up the coast to the Piedras Blancas elephant seal rookery, one of Summer's favorite places. She found watching the seals oddly comforting. They always did exactly what they were supposed to do, what was best for them as individuals and as a species. The human race could take lessons.

Route 1 took them along the coast, through small towns and past surf-pummeled rocks and beaches. Summer was driving her car after she found out Luke had gotten a ride to her house from a friend of Zac's. He must have been quite sure she'd forgive him, or he'd have had to walk a long way home.

At the rookery, they parked in the designated lot and followed the crowd onto the viewing platform set over the beach, where the animals lay by the dozens, females and pups and bulls, an impressive mass of life crowding the sand.

"I'm warning you, Luke." Summer gestured to the animals. "It's mating season. You might see some crazy action."

"No way." Luke surveyed the animals beneath them. "But they have babies now."

"They're just weaned. Then the bulls have to impregnate the females for next season."

"A man's work is never done."

"Ha!" Summer snorted. "The females are the ones doing all the work. Those pups gain ten pounds a day."

"Yeah?" Luke stepped closer and they listened to the deep belches of the males, the croaks of the moms and the high-pitched barks of the weaned pups, their arms touching. "So who did the housework in your family? Your mom? Did your dad help?"

Summer stiffened, then made herself relax. For better or worse, she had come to trust Luke a lot more, and he might as well know where she came from. "My parents had a pretty traditional work split."

When they did any work.

"Hey, sorry, I forgot you don't like talking about your

family." He turned to her, wind tousling his hair, his full mouth slightly pursed. "Never mind, then."

"It's okay." She had no idea why now, when they were standing near seals—which, face it, smelled really terrible—she was suddenly fantasizing about Luke kissing her. "I don't mind so much now."

"No? That's cool. Thanks, Summer." He smiled and nudged her with his shoulder. "My dad did everything. You know, Mom would have had a hard time helping, being dead and all."

"Luke." She was horrified. "You can't joke about that."

"Sure I can. But I know, that was bad." He put his arm around her for a brief squeeze. "Sometimes you get so sick of the pain that humor is a relief."

She nodded, her shock dissolving into sympathy. "There are probably as many ways of dealing with grief as there are people dealing with it."

"Probably. How do you cope?"

Summer frowned. She was grieving the pleasant carefree childhood she never got. Parents who would love her and sacrifice for her, who'd try hard not to spoil her and secretly enjoy it when they failed. Who cared enough about being good role models to keep trying when their efforts fell short. "I've never thought about it."

"What do you do when you're sad?"

"I go for a run. Or I clean. Mostly I clean." She laughed. "Doesn't that make me sound exciting?"

"Whoa, yeah, you are one crazy girl." He nudged her again. "Trust me, it's healthier than acting out."

"Look." Summer pointed. One of the enormous bulls, trunklike nose swinging, was heaving his incredible bulk along the sand at an astounding speed, chasing a squealing female, who was trying as hard as possible to get away from him.

"Aw, isn't that sweet." Luke cracked up, leaning into Summer to get a better view. "So romantic, huh? Look at her go!"

Summer giggled. "If someone was coming after me like that I'd run, too."

"How about if I was chasing after you?"

Oh, gosh. Just when she was about to go giddy at the thought of Luke trying to seduce her, he winked. She reminded herself that this was his autoflirt mechanism, not to be taken seriously.

"Hmm." She pretended to consider the concept. "Nope. Wouldn't work. It's not my style."

"It does lack subtlety."

"Have you ever had a serious girlfriend?"

He burst out laughing, harder than she'd ever seen him.

"What?" She had no idea what was so funny. "What did I say?"

"Sorry." He got himself under control. "It's just that you asked me that right after I talked about chasing you like a horny elephant seal. Like, 'Seriously, Luke? Have you ever even *had* a girlfriend?'"

Summer cracked up. "No, I definitely didn't mean that."

"To answer your question, no." He turned back to the seals, blushing. "I've dated around, nothing has ever really stuck. I probably need to grow up."

His admission surprised her. "Well, you have time. It's not like you're fifty and still haven't."

"What about you?"

"Do *I* need to grow up?" She'd had to grow up way too soon. "No, I'm perfect."

"How nice for you. I was talking about boyfriends."

"I had a couple. I mentioned them before. They were a little…rough."

His head jerked around, all laughter gone from his face. "With you?"

"No, no, not like that." She got a thrill from his protectiveness, even knowing she could take care of herself just fine, and pretty much always had. "One sold drugs. The other one stole. Took me a while to catch on, then when I did, I got out. That was it for me as far as boyfriends. Double fail."

"Well, you know, Summer, you still have time. It's not like you're fifty."

"So true!" She watched the seals cooling themselves, using their flippers to toss sand onto their backs, though the air was a pleasant temperature to her. Everything was pleasant to her right now. She was starting to realize how lonely she'd been without realizing it, keeping herself frenetically busy to hide the fact that she didn't have an intimate relationship in her life. Certainly not with her family after she'd moved out. As far as they were concerned, she was either selfish or a traitor or both. And she'd hardly seen Janine since she got her new boyfriend months ago.

"So you want to go somewhere that smells better?"

"Sure." She turned with Luke to walk back to the car. "Has Zac taken you to Hearst Castle yet?"

"Um, no. Not yet." He was speaking carefully.

"Not in the mood for a castle?"

"Honestly, Summer?" He touched her arm. "I just want to hang out with you somewhere we don't have to think about anything else. Like on a beach that doesn't smell like a seal sewer. Or at a coffee shop that isn't Slow Pour. Or, I don't know…"

"All of that sounds nice." Her voice came out low and shy.

"Cool." He took her hand and her heart started beating

faster again, plus a funny pressure swelled in her chest. She guessed it was just going to be that way around him until her infatuation faded or he broke her heart.

"Thank you for coming over today, Luke. I would have been too proud and too stubborn to apologize first. Seems like a stupid waste of time now." She liked the way his hand felt wrapped around hers. Such a little thing but it carried big emotional weight. "Though if you'd come into Slow Pour while I was working, I wouldn't have been able to stay mad for long."

"Yeah, well, maybe I am growing up a little." He moved away to smile at her, stretching their arms, then came back closer.

"Not always a bad thing." Summer smiled back. The pressure in her chest increased, and she suddenly understood exactly what it was.

She wanted to tell him her secret. She trusted him that much.

"I'm studying psychology. In case you wanted to know. As soon as I can I'm going to enroll full-time at Cal Poly." Her words rushed out and she was immediately anxious, as if she'd done something terrible and irrevocable, like push someone off a cliff.

"That's great." He squeezed her hand. "Good for you."

And…

That was it.

Summer nearly laughed. Why had she thought telling Luke would be a big deal? She might as well have told him what she had for breakfast, or that she was thinking of changing her hairstyle. Everyone went to college in his world. He had no reason to think she was extraordinary or daring to accomplish it in hers.

He'd also therefore have no reason to mock her, or to

tell her she couldn't possibly make it through the program. He had no reason to expect her to fail.

And it hit her that some of her attraction to this charming, funny man-boy was that around Luke, she already felt like the woman she wanted to become.

10

COLD. WHY WAS his room so cold? Zac reached for the extra blanket he kept at the bottom of his bed.

No blanket.

What was that noise?

He opened one eye. It was barely light outside.

He blinked to clear his vision and focused on…mmm, a female breast. Waves tumbled gently onto the sand behind him. His lips curved in a smile.

Oh, yeah.

He moved closer to Chris, who turned away, curling up against him.

Last night had been everything he'd fantasized and more. He'd been able to cut nearly all the way through the weird straitjacket she'd strapped herself into and connect to the fiery, funny woman he was so crazy about.

She'd cut through his straitjacket, too. Lying with her after having one of the most astounding orgasms of his life, he'd been able to open up a little, tell her something of what he was feeling, with amazing results: it hadn't killed him.

What's more, she was still here, so he hadn't scared her away. Now he was daring to hope his plan was going to work, that under the guise of a casual fling Chris would discover her feelings ran deeper than she thought. Maybe deep enough to keep the relationship going long-distance, or, if he got into Columbia, very short-distance.

That was the dream, anyway. He was getting way ahead of where they were now. He should take a page from her Zen book and concentrate on the moment.

Like that her hair smelled faintly of flowers.

Like that her legs were tangled with his.

Like that her incredibly firm and shapely ass was pressed against his groin.

He should let her sleep, but…

She stirred, letting out a faint whimper, then adjusted her body more firmly against his.

Zac stifled a groan. His flesh was definitely willing. Come to think of it, so was his spirit.

He moved his hand in a slow caress up her stomach, covering one of her beautiful breasts, feeling the nipple harden against his palm.

She whimpered again.

Drawing his hand down her stomach, he threaded his fingers into the curls between her legs. She stiffened in his arms.

"Good morning." He pushed into the dampness he'd tasted and thrust into and adored over most of the night.

"Mmmph."

He grinned, wondering if she was always slow to start in the mornings. So much he didn't know about her, so much he wanted to find out. "Did you sleep well?"

"Mmm-hmm."

He singled out her clitoris with the tip of one finger and circled it slowly.

"Zac."

"Yes, Chris." His finger moved farther into her, encountering moisture, which made his cock harden even more painfully.

"What are you doing?"

"I'm saying good morning."

"That's how you do it?" He could hear the smile in her voice, which only encouraged his exploration, while his cock was reduced to begging.

"Why, is there another way?"

"Jeez." She giggled. "You are such a guy."

His finger, slippery from her wetness, found and circled her clitoris again. "Want me to change?"

"Mmm, no, don't change." She arched back against him. He slid his penis into the gap at the top of her thighs, pushing to rub back and forth against her sex, making both of them groan at the pleasure. "I like you the way you are."

"'Kay." He couldn't handle more than one syllable. She'd started playing with her own breasts, stroking them, manipulating her nipples, and it was making him a little nuts.

"Zac."

"Whuh?"

She giggled, squeezing her thighs together, practically making his eyes roll back in his head. "Trouble speaking, dear?"

"Mhripghtp."

She rolled onto her stomach, grabbed a pillow and pushed it under her hips, tilting that gorgeous ass up high. There was enough dawn light to see darkness between her firm, shapely cheeks. "Maybe this will help?"

He groaned involuntarily, grabbed a condom from their depleted stash under the pillow—which, thankfully, hadn't been disturbed during the night—and had it on in record time.

"Brr. It's cold, Zac." She pretended to shiver, her voice low and sultry. "Warm me up."

"Ungh." He was on his knees between her thighs already, one hand on her hip, the other on his erection, ready to guide it into heaven.

She arched her back, tipping her pelvis farther toward him. He brought his cock to her soft lips and rubbed up and down the pink crevice, loving the sounds she made, the way she wiggled back toward him, pushing her bottom higher, wanting him inside her.

Applying gentle pressure, he watched his cock slowly disappear, inch by inch, her inner walls squeezing him, until he was fully inside. *Oh, man.* He stopped there, breathing fast, loving this moment of total connection before movement would escalate his lust toward its inevitable explosion and retreat.

Chris turned and met his eyes, hers shadowed by near darkness that turned her soft beauty mysterious and enticing. Tenderness mixed with desire so strongly he could only gaze back at her, wondering if she was the love of his life and what the hell he would do if she was.

Then she tossed her head so her hair swung over one perfect naked shoulder, pulling her hips forward and back, and desire won. He moved inside her, pleasuring her, pleasuring himself, wishing he was lying over her, gazing deeply into her eyes, able to tell her everything he felt.

Still too soon.

Frustration made him push harder, jolting her body. She rose up onto her arms, meeting his thrusts, uttering guttural cries that fueled his excitement until he was afraid he'd spin out of control.

"Zac." Her hand moved between her legs. She rubbed frantically as he pumped her until she stiffened and

gasped. Immediately he stopped holding back, let the orgasm sweep over him, aware of her muscles contracting around him as she came with him, aware of the softness of her skin, the fresh cool air around them, the regular splash and gurgle of the waves, wanting to capture and hold every aspect of the moment close in his memory.

Slowly he came down, regretfully, knowing they'd have to pack up and leave soon, leave behind this perfect bubble of passion and togetherness.

He pulled out of her, wanting Chris in his arms, face-to-face, wanting to ask what she was feeling, if her emotions had changed after their amazing night together.

Of course he did nothing like that, just gathered her to him and lay there as if he was only experiencing oh-baby-you-were-great afterglow.

"Mmm, Mr. Arnette, I have to say the benefits of being your friend are con-*sid*-erable."

He forced a laugh at the unintentional jab. In his view, what they'd shared had taken them way beyond friends. Even friends who were lovers. But he'd have to be patient. "Yeah? Think you might want to be this friendly again sometime?"

"Most definitely." She did sound happier and more relaxed than he'd heard her in a long time. "I love doing this with you. It's like… It's so…"

He waited eagerly. Fantastic? Incredible? Life changing?

"Nonthreatening."

Ouch. "Uh…yeah, wow, Chris. Every guy's dream after a long night of sex is to be told he's not threatening."

"I'm serious." She stretched luxuriously, making him want to pounce on her again. "I feel so comfortable with you. Like, amazingly comfortable."

He smiled. Of course she did. Because they were really, really good together. "Why do you think that is?"

Chris narrowed her eyes suspiciously. "You're smirking again. That means there's something going on in your head that you're not telling me."

"No, no, nothing like that." He made his smile as innocent as possible. "Go on."

"Well…a couple of things. First, I know you'll laugh, but I do think my experience at the Peace, Love and Joy Center has changed me."

Zac gritted his teeth. She was giving credit for how good they were together to some New Age BS yoga studio?

"And in this situation with you, I don't feel any expectations I have to live up to. I don't have to be the perfect partner."

His irritation dissolved into protective sympathy that any guy had made her feel that way—or even that she had to feel that way all on her own. He liked things black, white and organized. You needed clean water in a village. If there wasn't any, you found a way to bring it in. If you had storm overflow too often, you found new places for the water to go. But Chris's brain seemed to have much more complex reactions. It was obvious she'd struggled through life a great deal more than her outward control and competence let on.

"Of course you don't need to be perfect." He stroked her hair, keeping his voice light. "Perfection is boring."

"You think so?" She sighed. "I'm a perfectionist. Always have been. My parents, too. Eva was the lucky one in the family. She was sloppy and careless and fun from the moment she was born. She surprised and enchanted people. I have always felt completely predictable beside her. But then, that's what my parents raised me to be."

Zac nodded, wanting to ride in on his white horse and slay her demons. But he knew she'd have to put those to rest by herself. "I had a best friend growing up who was incredibly charming and passionate and cool. So I know that feeling. Next to him I was the too-big, slow-moving dork."

"I think you're charming and cool." She gave him a come-hither smile. "And I *know* you are passionate."

He dropped a thank-you kiss on the top of her head. "I know Eva admires you, but I bet she envied you, too, in a lot of ways."

"Grass is always greener?" Chris shrugged. "Maybe. But she is what she is, and always has been. She's done really well and is incredibly happy, and here I am, supposedly the daughter who's got it all together, and I'm still trying to figure so much out."

Here was his opportunity. But he'd have to tread carefully. "She's always been herself, Chris. But so have you. And you are also doing really well and will be incredibly happy someday, too."

She turned her head toward him, and where he expected her to bristle as she always did and insist she had changed and would continue to change, she just looked thoughtful and slightly troubled in a way that made him ache.

"I think I know what you're saying." Her fingertip touched his forehead, trailed down his nose and ran lightly over his lips. "I take it you're not that into my wig, huh?"

He laughed, relieved she wasn't upset. "I don't think it would fit me. But I love your tattoo."

"You saw that?"

He stroked the tiny phoenix on her left side under her

arm. "In case you didn't notice, I've been studying your body thoroughly."

"Mmm, I did notice."

He continued stroking her, listening to the waves, watching the dawn sky brighten, feeling their time together slipping away, minute by minute.

"So, Zac, I've been thinking."

"Yes?"

"About Valentine's Day."

Zac froze for a microsecond before he reminded himself to keep breathing. Was she going to say she wanted to hang out with him on Valentine's Day? Immediately he began thinking beyond boxes of chocolate, poetry and bouquets of roses to something that would represent his feelings without being too clichéd or scaring her.

"Yeah, I'd like to do something at Slow Pour."

"Okay." At Slow Pour? What kind of wildly romantic date was that? Unless she meant after hours, when the shop was dark and deserted.

"I've never really thought much of the holiday. I mean, really, do you need a calendar to tell you when to be romantic?"

"Nope." He was barely listening, thinking hard about Valentine's Day with Chris, and how far he could push—

"But Eva's doing a really nice event at NYEspresso, and I think I could do more with the shop on that day. What do you think?"

Oh.

Zac barely kept himself from growling. He was not doing the patience thing so well. It was a good sign that Chris wanted to celebrate a day of romance instead of ignoring it.

"I think a bigger event sounds great. What were you thinking of doing?" He snapped his fingers. "I know. You want me to dress up in a diaper and fairy wings with a bow and quiver of arrows and shoot your customers."

"Oh, that would be adorable!" She clapped her hands gleefully. "But no, not in a million years."

"I'm seriously disappointed."

"Uh-huh." Chris turned onto her side, absently stroking his chest. "I've got some decorations and special bakery items on order. But I want to do something bigger, something that will attract attention to the store, that will really spark interest."

"Set it on fire?"

She rolled her eyes, giggling. "You are such a help."

"Give away engagement rings?"

One dark eyebrow lifted. "You paying?"

"Um." He pretended to consider. "No."

"But maybe…" She frowned in concentration, then gasped, her face lighting. "I know! I could give away coffee for a year to any couple who gets engaged at Slow Pour on Valentine's Day!"

Immediately, even knowing he was being totally ridiculous, Zac imagined himself kneeling at her feet, offering Chris a ring. She'd be shocked at first, then her expression would clear and soften. Tears would run down her cheeks and she'd open her mouth and say—

"I am brilliant!" Chris rose to sitting. "Why didn't I think of this before? People will want to come from all over to hang out at Slow Pour in case someone proposes. And of course while they're waiting, they'll need coffee and food to tide them over. I can rent a tent for the front area and set up more tables, triple the pastry and drink orders, have my supplier deliver extra coffee. God, only if there's enough time. Let's see…"

"Chris."

"I have a week, right? Today is Saturday and Valentine's Day is next Saturday. I should still have time to get an article in the *Tribune*, because of course they'd want to cover this, then I'll post an article in the *Carmia Chronicle* online, put up posters around town…"

"*Chris.*"

"Mmm?" She swung her legs over the edge of the bed, propping her hands behind her to push herself onto the sand.

Zac dived after her and brought her back onto the bed so she was lying half under him. "You're not going anywhere yet."

"But I have to start—"

"The sun's not even up." He waggled his eyebrows menacingly. "And I've got the car keys."

She glared up at him. "You're holding me hostage?"

"Yes." He challenged her with a what-are-you-going-to-do-about-it stare. Five seconds later, the soft beauty of her eyes emasculated his stare, and he lowered his head, unable to keep from kissing her.

God, he was a sap. She deserved to win that one. Except instead of celebrating his capitulation, she wound her arms around his neck and responded eagerly.

Minutes later, he discovered all over again that it was virtually impossible to stop kissing Chris once he'd started. Every time he pulled back, he'd catch sight of her lips and think of another spot he might not have tasted enough. Or he'd catch her looking as if she were about to speak, or tensing as if she wanted to move, and he'd have to nip that in the bud in case she suggested they get out of bed.

He'd desired women before, but never with this combination of lust and tenderness, or with such an awareness of the soul within the body. He'd always prided himself on not having a scoring mentality, but this was a whole new dimension of feeling.

It thrilled him that Chris was back, in all her fiery overachiever glory and passion. He'd like to think he had something to do with that.

But with Ames likely to get a job offer this week, Chris's immersion in this new project meant Zac might not have enough time before she left for New York to convince her she belonged with him.

11

"Thanks very much." Chris punched off the phone in her office and pumped a fist in the air. The Valentine's event, conceived way too late to pull it off, was nevertheless on its way to being pulled off. The *Tribune* was sending someone out to interview her tomorrow, and the story would run Wednesday, plenty of time for some coffee-loving man—or maybe a woman—to make plans to propose at Slow Pour.

All Chris needed to make the event a success was one couple. She had no illusions that a coffee shop was the ultimate make-lifetime-memories place. But someone would go for it, maybe a couple who'd been living together for a while, for whom the commitment to marriage would be a mutual decision, not a surprise ooh-he-popped-the-question moment. After all, free coffee for a year added up to decent savings; the engaged couple could take a honeymoon cruise somewhere and only pay for one ticket with the amount of money they saved on coffee. Not bad. Chris would be sure to mention that in the interview.

She couldn't believe things were going so well. After realizing that what she really wanted and needed was this friends-with-benefits relationship with Zac, she seemed to grow calm and steady all on her own. No longer did she have to breathe consciously in order to regain control of her emotions or mood. Nor did she have to force herself to try to accept something she wasn't predisposed to accept. Colors suddenly seemed brighter, the air fresher—gosh, could you believe it, chirping cartoon birds followed her wherever she went!

Okay, now she was just being ridiculous.

Bottom line: instead of having to work at finding calm, it now seemed to come from inside her. It was a different calm, too. She felt more alive and energized, filled with a deep joy. Maybe Eva was right and she had been depressed before.

All she knew was that this felt absolutely wonderful. She had spent the most erotic, passionate, fantastic night of her life on Friday and well into Saturday, in a beachfront cabana in a private cove—who ever got to do *that*?—with Zac, and she still felt entirely stable and in control. She wasn't worried about whether he'd call her or not, she had no need to wonder where this relationship was going… It was all so perfect.

When the inevitable happened and Eva called to tell her Ames had gotten a job offer, which might happen very soon, she'd be able to say goodbye to Zac and go home to New York renewed and refreshed.

She couldn't ask for anything better.

Her cell phone rang. It was Zac.

A warm thrill coursed through her. "Hey, there."

"Hello."

That's all it took. One word in that deep voice, and she was a Krispy Kreme doughnut—all jelly inside.

"Zac, you shouldn't be calling me at work."

"I know. I shouldn't be calling you from work, either.

But if I don't hear your voice at least once every three hours I start having painful withdrawal symptoms."

She snorted, more pleased than she wanted to admit. "Anything embarrassing?"

"My colleagues are a little disturbed by the howling, yeah."

Chris turned to hide her giggles from an elderly couple sitting near the counter. As shop manager, she should only be conducting business calls in front of customers.

"So, Chris, what are you doing tonight?"

"Not seeing you."

He inhaled sharply. "Oh, I'm sorry. That sounds like a really dull evening."

It did. She admitted it. "We have a date Wednesday."

"But Wednesday isn't tonight." He could not sound any sexier.

"No, it's not."

"Agreed, then. I'll pick you up after work. Will you be home?"

Chris frowned, wanting desperately to say yes, but feeling as if seeing him every day might…

Might… Um…

Wait, hadn't she just finished telling herself that everything in her life was under control, especially in regard to Zac? What exactly was she afraid of?

She didn't know. But something deep inside her was sending out warning signals.

"I'll behave myself, Chris, I promise. I'll wait ten, no, fifteen, no, *twenty* seconds before I start taking your clothes off."

She rolled her eyes. "Impressive."

"I really, really want my mouth on your incredibly beautiful breasts again." His voice dropped to a murmur. "And I want to slide my hand down your pants and touch you all over."

Oh, my. She had to swallow before she could speak. "I'm at work, Zac."

"After that I'll take off your panties so I can—"

"No, that won't work. You haven't taken off my pants yet." She waited in delight, knowing he'd tease her for being so precise.

"Oh, my God." Zac was laughing. "Even your *fantasies* have to be perfect?"

"Look, Zac, if you're going to do something, you have to—"

"She said he hasn't taken off her pants yet."

The elderly woman's voice made Chris whirl around in horror, to find the couple staring at her.

"I thought that's what she said." The man smiled and nodded approvingly. "Go on, go on. We don't mind."

Ew.

"Chris?" Zac sounded worried.

She spun back around, utterly mortified. "I have to go."

"Can I pick you up at five-thirty?"

"Uh…" Chris gestured helplessly. "*Yes*, okay."

"Good. I'll see you then."

She hung up the phone and stared at it. How did that happen? She wasn't supposed to see Zac until Wednesday, and that had felt like a very smart decision. Now…

A grin spread across her face. Now she was going to see him tonight, and that felt like a smarter one.

But—she glanced at the couple who, thank God, were back to drinking their coffee and reading their newspapers—absolutely no more phone calls about her pants coming down.

At least not at work.

The door to the café opened and Gus strode in, accompanied by a tiny blonde woman, who hung on to his arm as if she'd crumple if she let go.

"Hey, Chris, how's it going? I want you to meet Pammy." He gazed down adoringly at the blonde. "She *surfs*."

Chris smiled warmly. Wow! Had Gus found someone? This was great news. "Hi, Pammy."

"Hi, Chris. Gus has totally told me all about you." Pammy blinked up at him with puppy eyes, which made Gus puff out his chest, looking even hotter and goofier than usual. "He says you're the best."

"*Second* best." Gus leaned down to rub her nose with his.

Chris's smile turned slightly sick. She could only take so much goo. Of course, she'd just been discussing her panties in public. "Can I get you guys some Suja Juice?"

"Wow!" Pammy stared at Chris as if she'd just performed a miracle. "That's totally what we came in for! It's like you *knew*."

Uh-huh. No question. Gus and Pammy were perfect for each other. "It's all Gus ever orders."

"I'll go with my usual, Berryoxidant. Pammy?"

"Um…you decide for me."

"Okay. For you…" Gus waggled his eyebrows. "Honeybush Peach."

"Coming up." Chris turned to get the juice before she started gagging.

"Yo, so, Chris, have you seen Bodie? The dude didn't show up at the beach today and he's not answering his phone."

"Haven't seen him since Friday night." Chris put the bottles on the counter. "He dropped me off and said he was going back to the A-Frame."

"It's weird. He's never missed a session without letting me know." Gus held up his fingers half an inch apart. "I'm this close to calling the police."

"Hmm." Chris frowned, trying to look concerned, but thinking the police wouldn't be too impressed by one broken surf date. "I'd wait another day. He's probably busy, or his phone died, or both."

"That's exactly what I said!" Pammy stroked Gus's arm. "I'm sure he's fine, sweetie."

"It's just freaky, is all. Oh, well." He passed the Honeybush Peach to Pammy and hoisted his Berryoxidant. "Ready to catch some waves, babe?"

"Totally." She clinked her bottle to his and turned to Chris. "Nice to meet you."

"Same here." She watched them leave, hoping the relationship worked out for Gus, feeling a little wistful about their blissful coupledom. Not that it was right for her just now. But someday she'd like a guy to go that crazy over her. Gus was so sweet.

The next couple of hours were fairly quiet, and she was able to escape to the office to work up a fun poster for the Valentine's event, which she then emailed to a print shop in San Luis Obispo for overnight printing. In the morning, she'd pick up the posters and deliver them to a company that had promised to plaster the area for a reasonable price. Terrified she'd run out of food, she'd also scheduled a run to a big-box store for bags of everyone's favorite Valentine candy, along with extra decorations.

Chairs, tent, extra tables—was she forgetting anything? Something for the prospective groom—or bride—to kneel on? Romantic music to play throughout the day? Yes, and yes, add those to the big-box run.

She heard the front door of the shop open and bolted up.

"Hi, Chris." Summer's voice floated back. "I'm here. I'm so sorry."

Startled, Chris glanced at the clock. It was after two. She'd never known Summer to be late. "Don't worry about it. I had plenty to do here."

"Yeah? It's been busy?" The younger woman appeared in Chris's doorway, eyes sparkling, cheeks flushed. "Anything I can do to help?"

"No, actually, I think it's all under control." She described the event briefly, delighted to watch Summer react with genuine enthusiasm.

Chris gathered up her lists in a neat pile, wondering how far she could pry. "So did you have a good morning?"

"Yeah, it was fun." Summer grabbed her Slow Pour apron from the wooden peg on the wall outside the office and lowered it over her head. "Luke and I hung out in San Luis Obispo."

"Oh, how…nice." Chris wasn't so sure. Summer had admitted to Chris sometime ago that she made bad dating choices. Now she was hanging out with a bar brawler? But then…Luke was Zac's brother. He couldn't be all bad. At least, she hoped not. "He seems like a nice kid."

"Yeah." Summer blushed ruby red. "Yeah, he's nice."

"Okay, Summer." Chris pushed back her chair from the desk. "What's going on?"

"What do you mean?"

"Summer…"

"Okay, okay." She smiled her fantastic white-toothed smile. "He's great, actually. I'm still being careful, but underneath the attitude he seems really solid. He's amazingly honest and he can be really sweet."

"And the whole arrest thing…?"

Summer pressed her lips together. "Like I said, I'm

being careful. So far, though, it seems like he's working hard to change. And it seems like the kids he hung out with back east were jerks. Plus, I don't know...I feel safe with him. It makes me realize I never did with the other guys."

"That's wonderful." Chris nodded, understanding more than Summer probably realized. "You'll be a good influence, too."

"We'll see." Summer tied the apron ties behind her back and gave Chris a sly smile. "So. What's going on with Zac?"

Chris faked surprise. "Whatever do you mean, Summer?"

"Chris..."

Chris grinned, feeling herself blushing. "Things are fine. Casual, but good. I feel great."

"Same here." Summer put a hand to her chest. "I feel like I'm coming to life or something. I'm so enjoying this. And him."

Chris nodded. Yeah, she got that, too. "I'm very happy for—"

"Hello?"

Yikes. Chris hadn't heard the front door open. "Customer."

"I'm on it." Summer disappeared around the corner.

Chris locked up her desk, took off her apron and grabbed her jacket. She'd go home, take a nap and a nice bath and get ready for her unexpected date tonight.

Boy, did she *love* this feeling of anticipation, knowing that her emotions and her spirit were not going to be ground down and hijacked by the agonies of falling in love. Everything about this relationship felt so completely right.

She walked out into the shop, where one of the most

gorgeous women she'd ever seen was standing at the counter. Voluptuous, dark and exotic-looking. Maybe a hint of Spanish or Italian blood? Brazilian?

Immediately Chris started wondering if she'd seen her in a movie or on TV. California was full of those types, and you never knew when they'd show up. One day Jennifer Aniston had walked in for an espresso. Chris had nearly dropped dead of shock.

"You must be Chris." The woman's voice was low and musical. Was anything not perfect about her? She couldn't be a movie star if she knew Chris's name.

"Yes, I'm Chris."

"Jackie Cawling." She held out her hand, which wasn't perfectly manicured. Ha! Human after all.

"Nice to meet you." Awkward pause. Was the name supposed to mean something to her? "Are you from the *Tribune*?"

She looked taken aback. "No, no, I'm a friend of Zac's."

"Oh, yes. Hi." She searched her brain, trying to figure out if Zac had mentioned a Jackie, and came up empty.

"We met in the Peace Corps, in Kenya?" She waited expectantly, as if this prompt should have cleared everything up.

It didn't.

"Ah." Chris nodded politely.

"He didn't mention me?" Her full lips curved in a smile. "I'm staying at his place."

Huh?

"Uh. No." She felt stupid. Why did Jackie know about Chris but Chris had no idea about her? "Or maybe he did and I… No, he didn't."

"Oh. Well, that's weird." She laughed, a sexy, low

laugh that made Chris want to growl at her. "You stayed at my friend's cabin on Friday night."

"Oh. Right." She searched her brain again. Zac had said friend of a friend, but had never elaborated. Nor had he mentioned the woman was sleeping at his house.

As was Luke.

How many bedrooms…

No, come on. Zac wasn't the juggle-women type.

"Anyway, I came in today because Zac doesn't have an espresso machine at his house and I'm addicted. And because I wanted to meet the woman he's so taken with."

"Oh, how nice." That felt *much* better. If Zac had told her they were involved, he certainly wasn't playing games.

"Zac is *very* special to me." One of Jackie's perfect brown brows lifted. "We go back a long way. We've been through a lot together."

And…now she felt worse again. Jackie and Zac used to be a couple, probably serious. It was so obvious Jackie might as well have screamed it right into Chris's face.

"That's great." Chris was not rising to the bait. "Are you having a good visit?"

"Oh, yes. We always have a great time together. He's one of those people I can see rarely, but when we're back together it's like we were never apart."

Just. Shut. Up.

The enormity of the gap between this woman's long, intimate friendship with Zac and the silly fling Chris was having with him was choking her. This woman would know things about Zac that Chris never would. She'd probably been touched by his hand with real love, had been gazed at with deep tenderness, had laughed with him, had felt they truly belonged together.

Maybe she still did.

An iron hand seemed to have reached into Chris's body, taken a handful of her guts and was twisting the life out of them. She could hardly breathe for the pain.

She was jealous. Violently jealous. Catfight jealous. She wanted all those things from Zac and she wanted this woman never to have had them.

Which meant her triumph over the success of this relationship, her belief that it was light, easy, under control, that her feelings for Zac would be easily left behind when she moved back to New York—all that was yet another way she was lying to herself.

Eva's prediction had come true: Chris was falling in love with Zac.

12

"Before I hang up, I have to tell you something."

"Yeah? What's that?" Zac had just stepped out of the shower at work. Nice perk to working at a big firm—they had a gym and locker room for employees. He'd left his desk early so he'd have time to clean up and shave before picking Chris up at five-thirty. Luke had called to say he and Summer were hanging out at Summer's house, and Jackie had left Carmia to work her way up the coast before returning to Los Angeles and the world beyond.

Which meant his place would be wide-open for him and Chris.

Yeah, he was heartbroken about that.

"I stopped by Slow Pour on my way out of town for an espresso."

Zac froze. Had he ever told Chris about Jackie being in town? They'd been in bed most of the day Saturday. During that time, Jackie had not exactly been uppermost in his mind. He'd devoted Sunday to catching up with his friend, taking her around Carmia, and they'd stayed up talking well into the wee hours of Monday morning, until he'd dragged himself to bed, knowing he had to be up early.

And now…it looked as if he'd pulled a classic Dumb Guy move.

"Hang on, Jackie, let me put you on speaker." He adjusted the settings on his phone. "Okay, I'm here. You stopped at Slow Pour? How was that?"

"You were absolutely right."

Zac stopped with his hand on his shaving kit. Right about what? That Jackie would like Chris? That Chris would like Jackie? That Chris was preparing to kill him because he hadn't mentioned he had an old girlfriend sleeping over?

"I was?"

"Yup. *Great* cup of coffee."

Zac snorted. "Just what I wanted to hear."

Jackie laughed her deep, brassy laugh. "I know, that was mean. Yes, I wanted to meet this woman who has you all turned upside down."

Zac fished out his razor. *And?* "How did that go?"

"Very interesting. For one thing, she's beautiful."

"I know." He secured the towel around his waist and stepped to the mirror over the row of sinks, understanding Jackie was enjoying her moment but wishing she'd get to the point.

"And she gives off this great contrasting vibe, like if someone cracked her supercontrolled exterior there'd be this boiling mass of energy and insecurity and passion."

"I know that, too." He squirted out a puff of shaving cream and started spreading it onto his face. So far it didn't sound as if Chris had gone banshee on him. But then, as Jackie said, she was a master of self-control.

Except when he had his hands on her…

"But I bet you *didn't* know…"

Zac stopped with his razor in midair. "Didn't know…"

"That she's on her way to falling in love with you, if she's not already there."

Zac put down the razor, his heart thumping. "What makes you say that?"

"If she was in this just as a friend with benefits, she would not have wanted to rip my head off, stick it on a spear and dance around it."

"Ah." Zac forced a chuckle, trying to figure out where this was going. "She happened to mention that?"

"I saw it in her eyes."

Uh-oh.

"Oh, come on." He picked up the razor again. "You can't tell all that from someone's eyes. At least not the spear part. What the hell did you do to get her that pissed off?"

"It was fine at first. She was all warm and welcoming until I told her I was staying with you. Which, my wonderful brainless friend, you forgot to mention to her."

"Yeah." Zac drew the razor down his cheek, cursing his bad judgment. "But it was never the right time to say, 'By the way, I have an old girlfriend staying at my place.'"

"Bad call."

He didn't like the sound of that. "She can't think you and I are still together."

"I'm sure she doesn't. But she still got all frosty and bristly. And because I'm a nosy person, I made a point of talking about how long you and I had known each other and how much we'd been through together, and how *special* you were to me, blah, blah, blah."

"Jackie…" He was not amused by that game.

"I knew you'd never do something sensible like ask her how she felt or tell her how you were feeling, so I figured I'd help move things along. I'm telling you, she was ready to set me on fire. If she wasn't totally crazy about you, why would she care what you and I meant to each other a long time ago?"

"Hmm." Zac's heart started going a little nutty in his chest. "Interesting logic."

"Well, then, of course I felt bad for putting her through that, so I made it clear nothing had happened between us in years, nor would it, and we ended with a nice chat and hugs all around. But I'm telling you, Zac, Chris is in love with you."

Thank God men didn't use straight razors anymore, or he would have cut his chin off. "She can't feel that strongly yet."

"Don't you?"

Yes. The answer hit him with simple clarity. It made no sense. They hadn't known each other long enough, they hadn't had time to discover each other's values, to know if they had the same rhythms and habits, all the things that made the difference between success and failure in a relationship. But he already knew he'd never felt this way about anyone else. Maybe it was just cowardice that had kept him from labeling the emotion.

He lowered the razor and stared at himself, face half covered in lather.

"I thought so." Jackie was clearly smug. "So, Zac, dear, my job here is done and I need to concentrate on driving. It was great to see you. Be good. Oh, and invite me to the wedding, okay?"

He laughed, said a warm goodbye, and urged her to call again soon, hardly aware of what he was saying.

Chris was in love with him? Of course, that was just Jackie's opinion, but she did have amazingly good intuition.

Around Zac, Chris had been determinedly casual, but

he had thought a few times that her guard had slipped, that her warmth might be more than affection, that the vulnerability in her eyes might signify a deeper emotion.

He'd been afraid of wishful thinking. He still was. It was hard to imagine that his plan might have worked this fast, that they could establish a solid foundation as a couple so they could remain one after she left.

His phone rang again; he glanced at it absently. It was Gus.

Sorry, Gus. Zac picked up his razor and went back to work.

He had a friends-with-benefits date to prepare for, with a woman who might be ready to admit she wanted more.

MEDITATING WASN'T WORKING. Deep breathing and relaxation weren't working. Positive visualization wasn't working. Medication might work, but Chris couldn't get to a doctor in time.

What had happened to the new her? Or the *new* new her? *Argh.* She might as well admit it. She hadn't changed, not truly, not deep down. She was herself all over again and always would be—anxious, anal-retentive and about as free-spirited as a robot.

Everyone had tried to tell her—Eva, Summer in her quiet way and, of course, Zac.

No amount of tattoos, piercings or wigs could make her into someone else. She'd tossed the wig the moment she got home from work. Ditto the ear cuffs and the temporary hair dye. The tattoo she couldn't erase, but she regretted ever getting it.

Okay, okay, she shouldn't beat herself up too much. For one thing, self-flagellation was extremely unconstructive. For another, she had a date with Zac in half an hour and she needed to calm down enough to figure out how to play this. Because she was Old Chris, and always would be Old Chris, she was going to think the problem through in a neat outline form.

Her options were the following:

One, pretend she was still only interested in the friends-with-benefits arrangement Zac wanted. She'd risk nothing that way, and keep her heart safe. She'd also probably spend the rest of her life wondering what would have happened if she'd told Zac she wanted more.

Two, she could admit to Zac that she wanted more and…

Subparagraph a) Zac could respond positively. That would be honest, which was generally a good idea, and could open the door to a richer and more intimate relationship, which, given that she wouldn't be here much longer, could be either short-term or long-distance, neither of which suited her.

Subparagraph b) Zac could respond negatively, bringing on rejection, humiliation and/or heartbreak, and ruining their chances for a long-term friendship.

Three, Chris could hint at her feelings and see how he reacted. If he seemed put off, she could easily back down. If he seemed pleased, she could push a little further. Repeat as needed. This was the wimpiest, safest and most practical option, which meant she'd probably go with it.

Up until a few months ago, she would have chosen that option without thinking.

Now? She wasn't sure about anything anymore.

Chris sighed and went to look at herself in the mirror for the dozenth time. She wasn't even sure about her outfit. The day was warm for February—California warm, in the seventies. She'd chosen a short flared black skirt with a rose pattern in corals, pinks and greens and a fit-ted white blouse with short sleeves and tucks down the front. On her feet, black strappy sandals.

Too country? Not sexy enough? Too formal? Too casual?

Oh, for crying out loud. She was officially exhausting herself.

This was what she was wearing. There. Decided. As for what to do and how to act around Zac, she'd make it up as she went along.

Done.

By the time Zac showed up half an hour later, she was calmer, thanks to a sustained effort to relax. The skills she'd learned at the Peace, Love and Joy Center were not totally wasted. Even if she'd never become a calm person or be able to live entirely in the moment, she certainly had a better ability to look inside herself and admit truths she might have previously denied.

And then there was the other thing, which no amount of meditating or looking inward could do for her. One look into Zac's blue eyes and her stress and angst began dissolving into pure pleasure. The fact that he grabbed her and kissed her as if he hadn't seen her for weeks didn't hurt, either.

"Hi." He rested his forehead against hers. "I missed you. How dumb is that?"

She laughed, taken aback. She hadn't expected emotion like that from Zac. "I'd say pretty dumb. Which must mean I'm pretty dumb, too."

"Yeah?" He brushed her hair back from her face, watching her with his steady, warm gaze. "Aren't we supposed to be take-it-or-leave-it with each other?"

"So we messed up this time." She shrugged. "We'll just make more of an effort to enjoy each other less."

"We can only try." He grasped her chin and brought

her mouth to his, kissing her leisurely until she felt that sweet jelly-doughnut thing happening again. "Uh-oh."

"What is it?" She sounded like a breathless fool.

Probably because she was one.

"I enjoyed that, too. Sorry, Chris."

She gave him a reproving look. "We'll have to stop, then. No more kissing."

"Yeah, forget that."

They stood smiling at each other like complete morons until Chris finally took a step back and broke the moron spell. "Want to come in?"

"Are Eva and Ames home?"

"Does it matter?" She giggled at his are-you-kidding-me expression. "They're out for dinner and not expected back for hours."

"Hours." He frowned, looking perplexed. "I guess it's kind of rude to celebrate that, huh."

"It is, but I'll join you." She gestured him into the living room. "How was work today, dear?"

He chuckled. "The usual. I had a weird call from Gus, though. Apparently he's misplaced Bodie."

"So he said. He came into Slow Pour today. With his new girlfriend."

"No way, really?"

"Yup. Pammy. She's adorable. They seem totally smitten." Chris put her iPod on shuffle, since she hadn't been able to decide on the perfect music for her mood. Because she hadn't even been able to decide what her mood was. "I haven't seen Bodie since we had dinner."

"Speaking of which, I made us a reservation for tonight at Ciopinot in San Luis Obispo. Fantastic seafood place. Sorry you won't be with Bodie again, but..."

"Oh, yeah, that'll be tough, but I'll struggle through

it. Thank you, Zac. It sounds wonderful." Except... "Do we have time for a drink first?"

"We do." He smiled suggestively. "Quite a bit of time. The reservation isn't until eight, which leaves us about two hours."

"Two hours of drinking?" She blinked sweetly. A Rubén Blades salsa number started up, filling the room with spirited, sensual sound. Almost unconsciously Chris started moving her hips to the beat. "Is that a good idea?"

"Oh, no." He took a step toward her, watching her shimmy with an oh-baby smile curving his lips. "Two hours of drinking is a terrible idea."

"I thought so." She kept dancing, feeling herself heat up at his prowling approach. "What could we do instead? Any ideas?"

"Oh, Chris." He sent her an incredibly sexy look. "Way, way too many."

"Hmm." She felt a sudden burst of happiness and an unexpected sense of power. Where that came from, she had no idea, but in a sudden fit of who-cares optimism, she decided to stop angsting and analyzing and just go with it. "Maybe I can help you narrow those down."

"I'd appreciate anything you can do."

"I'll start here." She unbuttoned two buttons of her blouse, increasing the side-to-side motion of her hips in time to the music, wishing she'd worn something she could rip off...until she noticed how intently Zac was watching her.

Instinctively, her fingers slowed down. She felt the smooth plastic of each button, felt it give when the hole stretched wide enough to set it free. Felt the brush of material over her skin as the shirt loosened and slipped off.

"Yeah." He pointed. "Yeah, I like that idea."

"I have more," she whispered. She unhooked her bra, releasing her breasts, nipples emerging into the cooler air.

"I *really* like that one." He was unbuttoning his own shirt, white woven cotton with a thin blue stripe. Under it he wore a soft, sleeveless undershirt that showed off his well-defined arms. Chris loved those arms around her, loved their power and the way they held her tightly against him. "How's this?"

"*Very* nice."

The brass section started a spirited solo. Zac's undershirt came off, stripped from the bottom up, slowly revealing his nicely muscled abdomen and chest, smooth and tempting to her fingers and tongue.

Not yet. She wanted to wait longer, to be even hungrier for him.

She kicked off one sandal, then the other. One-two, one-two.

He stepped out of his shoes and pulled off his socks. One-two-three-four.

The band let loose; Chris unfastened the waistband of her skirt and let it slide to the floor.

Zac unzipped his fly, rescued a condom from his pocket and held it between his teeth, giving her a fierce raised-eyebrow look that made her giggle.

One-ha! Two-ha!

Keeping his spirit of melodrama, she shimmied out of her panties, paused with them high over her head, and flung them across the room, encouraged by the conga drums.

Naked, one-two, and—*attack*!

They came together in the middle of the room in an embrace that nearly knocked them both over, kissing frantically, half laughing, half deranged with lust.

Chris turned her mind off, letting herself drown in

the physical sensations, the style and rhythm of the music, the warmth of his mouth, the smooth, wonderful feel of his skin against hers, chest to knee, the sexy aftershave-enhanced smell of that skin. His impressive erection prodded her lower belly, making it clear how much he wanted her.

She wanted him, too, more than just today and tomorrow, more than just once in a while.

They moved toward the bedroom and fell onto the bed, twisting around so Chris was on top. Hands over her head, she straddled his erection, gyrating to the music, flinging her head around, letting the beat completely take her over.

Without a drop of alcohol in her system, she felt drunk; without an ounce of any drug, she was high, full of so much life she was afraid she'd explode from the feelings and the joy of it.

The piece ended. An Artie Shaw big-band number came on, "Begin the Beguine," one of her mom's favorite songs. She'd forgotten it was on there. The moody clarinet rose and fell over a tropical beat, a different kind of sexy.

"Changeup." Zac held her hips and tumbled her to the side, following, his big body covering hers.

She wrapped her arms around his neck and stared into his eyes, loving their blue shade, their warmth, their openness, loving the connection that went deeper than any she'd had before. This man cared about her; he wanted only for her to be her own flawed self, to love and accept her flaws the way he had.

Wasn't that at the heart of what they taught at the Peace, Love and Joy Center?

Somehow she'd missed the mark, adopting a model of behavior and being that was too far outside of herself for her ever to internalize it. She'd been a perfectionist even in trying to throw off perfectionism.

Zac's wonderful, handsome face came down to hers for another long kiss that ignited more fires in her body... but also more longing in her heart.

She was ready to examine those emotions, to confront them honestly, to see, without the filter of analysis or rationalization, exactly what she felt for this man.

A lot.

"Chris." He said her name with such intensity, such depth of feeling, that she allowed herself to hope he was as far gone as she was.

From the other room, the big band finished an interlude and the clarinet resumed the elegant melody, crooning, crying, singing it out. Chris opened her legs, inviting Zac in, wanting them to join intimately with their bodies, as well as—someday, hopefully—with their hearts.

Zac lifted to roll on the condom.

During that brief pause, a few sensible and practical doubts crept into her thoughts. What was the point of falling hard for a man she'd soon be separated from? Maybe very soon? Wouldn't the pain be that much greater if she got in too deep now? Wouldn't it make sense to pull back now instead of forging ahead?

Chris thanked the thoughts politely for their intrusion and told them in no uncertain terms to get the hell out of her head, because she had a really hot and really wonderful man in bed with her, and many, many things to do with him.

She grinned up at him, gyrating to the jazzy tempo. "Let's begin this beguine, baby."

He laughed and moved back over her to flick his tongue firmly over her nipple, then closer to suckle her, tongue swirling around her areola, stoking the fires.

Under her fingers his hair was thick and soft and his back provided a glorious stretch of skin and muscle for her other hand to explore.

"Mmm, I love what you do to me, Zac."

"I'd like to keep doing it for a long, long time, Chris." He smiled into her eyes for several heart-pounding seconds before he bent to worship her other breast.

Chris bit her bottom lip. A long, long time? What did that mean? Today, in terms of minutes? Or over and over in terms of days stretching on into the future?

Shh. Quiet. Listen to the music. Love the man.

The man stroked his hand down between her breasts and over her belly to tangle his fingers in the curls between her legs, moving them in gentle exploration before sweeping his hand back up.

Then he moved it back down again, spreading her labia wide this time, lingering over her clitoris, sending a hot burst of arousal through her that caused her to arch up to his hand.

"Mmm. You can do that for a long, long time, too, Zac."

"I intend to." His warm hand slid up again, passed over one breast then the other, and slid back down, playing there, circling, rubbing...then he thrust a finger inside her, making her gasp with pleasure.

"You like that?"

"Oh...yes." She closed her eyes, letting him make love to her with one finger, then two, his thumb stopping now and then to tease her clitoris.

"Zac." She whispered his name with the same tenderness he'd used, feeling a swell of emotion that had only partly to do with the pleasure his fingers were giving her.

He moved down and his mouth replaced his thumb. His tongue swirled over her clit, bringing her up and up and…he stopped. She came down, panting, incredibly hot, incredibly disappointed. Until he resumed his magic and sent her spiraling back up toward a climax… and again, eased her gently down, his tongue resting, fingers going still inside her. Back up, then down, up, down, until she was shaking with frustration.

"Zac!" This time there was no tenderness in her voice, only demand for her release.

He lunged over her immediately, one hard thrust taking him in all the way. Chris cried out, nearly losing her mind at the pleasure. She spread her legs wider, drew her knees up to her shoulders, urging him to drive harder. He obliged her with strokes that shook the bed, made her grab at the headboard to keep from banging into it.

Then his thrusts slowed to a stop, though his breath still came hard. He lay still for a moment, until she registered that the music had changed again. "Make You Feel My Love."

Zac lifted his head, this time moving in an entirely different rhythm, a slow in and out, pausing to grind his hips over her clitoris while Adele's rough, throaty voice sang of love and comfort.

Chris hooked her legs over his, using the leverage to push back against him, slow in, slow out, gazing into his blue, blue eyes, thinking that she'd never felt this close to anyone, never allowed herself to be this wide-open. Not to anyone.

Zac.

He kissed her, took her lower lip into his mouth and sucked gently.

"Mmm." His back was long and lean under her fingers, his buttocks firm. She pushed her fingers into the muscle, feeling it contract as he moved.

His body tensed; his motion accelerated. Chris responded once more, her desire climbing, body gathering itself, reaching toward the climax, maybe this time…

He pulled out nearly all the way and slowly pushed just the tip of his cock in and out of her, stretching and teasing until she was so close, so close, not able to get over, but *so close*…

With a groan he thrust all the way back in, then again and again. She dug her fingers into his back, close to screaming, feeling the orgasm approaching inevitably now.

It tore into her, nearly unbearably intense, and she was yelling, *oh, oh, oh*, thrashing her head, completely out of control and letting herself be that way.

Zac tensed, shouting his own pleasure as he came with her.

The song finished. Another came on, and in an incredibly weird coincidence, it was "Afterglow" by INXS.

Slowly Chris returned to earth, breathing hard, blinking in a kind of stupefied trance. Slowly, she untangled her brain from the fading ecstasy and tuned in to the man on top of her, slumped and breathless.

This time when he raised his head to look down at her, she held nothing back, let him see her vulnerability, her passion, her awe of what they had done, her hope for what they might be able to do, given time.

Time.

"Zac."

"Chris."

They spoke together and both laughed, a little shaky, a little uncertain.

I love you.

No, it was too soon, the emotion unfairly influenced by the passion they'd just shared. These declarations needed to wait until she was sure, until…

No. To hell with caution. To hell with analysis and practicality and common sense. She wanted to say it now because she was feeling it deep down through her whole body and through her whole heart.

She opened her mouth to speak.

Zac opened his mouth to speak.

In a crazy intuitive flash, Chris thought he was about to tell her the same thing she was about to tell him.

Her phone rang, catching them both with their mouths open, ruining the mood and the moment. Zac kissed her and rolled to the side. "Did you want to get that?"

"No, I'll look later." She forced a smile, feeling cheated out of something potentially momentous and life altering, but also relieved. Zac might have been about to say, *thanks for the world's greatest orgasm.* Or to ask to use the toilet. In which case she would have sounded pretty stupid telling him she loved him. Maybe it was just as well.

Maybe.

She snuggled up against Zac's chest, inhaling his scent, concentrating on all the places their bodies were intersecting instead of on what might have been and whether or not it was a good idea.

"What time do you think it is?"

"I have no idea." Chris lifted her head, straining to see the clock by the bed, forgetting that Eva didn't have one. "I forgot we have a reservation. Hell, I forgot my name."

He stroked her hair, one of the best feelings in the world. "I know what you mean."

"I'll go check."

"Do you have to?"

"Yes." She rolled away from him, sat on the edge of the mattress and stretched luxuriously. "Because otherwise I'll worry."

His wonderful chuckle sounded behind her. "Of course you will."

Chris pushed off the bed. He didn't care if she was a mess sometimes. And maybe she didn't, either. Or shouldn't, anyway.

She padded into the hall to retrieve her phone from the pocket of her discarded skirt and brought it back into the room. "Just after seven. We've got plenty of time. And the call was from Eva. Wait, she texted me. Call me back ASAP."

"Go ahead." Zac slid out of bed and took her in his arms. "But first…"

Being kissed over and over and over by a man you'd just had amazing sex with was even better than having your hair stroked.

"Mmm." Reluctantly, she let him head for the bathroom, while she stood there like a moonstruck buffoon for about two minutes before she managed to calm down enough to dial her sister. "Hey, Eva, I got your message. Everything okay?"

"Are you with Zac?"

"Yes." She turned toward the door he'd left through. "Why?"

"Because the two of you better start getting serious."

Chris blinked. Had her sister been watching? "Really? Gee, I'll get right on it. Why do you say that?"

Zac came out of the bathroom. He stopped in the doorway, his head almost touching the top of the frame, body practically filling it, hands on his hips, looking her naked body up and down, his sexy lips curved in a smile.

She was crazy about him.

"Because, dear twin, Ames was offered the job this afternoon. They want him to start as soon as possible."

13

BODIE WOKE FROM a strange dream in which he was shackled to an iron bed with chains around his wrists and ankles.

He tried to scratch his balls, but there was a clanking, jingling noise and then his hand was brought up short.

What the—?

He *was* shackled to an iron bed with chains around his wrists and ankles.

Oh, yeah. The blonde he'd met at the A-Frame. What had started as sex with light bondage had turned serious. She'd taken him prisoner, chained him to this bed, unable to move without her permission, unable to eat, drink or pee without her permission, unable to *surf*!

Damn!

Gus would miss him. Gus knew Bodie would never miss a session. He'd call the cops. Someone would have seen him leaving the bar with her. Someone would be able to trace him here, wherever *here* was.

In the meantime, he was a prisoner, victim to her rough sexual games, some of which went on for hours.

The door to the room opened. It was her, Gail, wearing the full getup—a black leather bikini, elbow and knee pads, and a black leather mask across her eyes. He'd thought she was pretty hot at the A-Frame, but he'd had no idea what she was capable of.

"Good morning, slave." She cracked her whip and climbed up onto the bed. He groaned, briefly closing his eyes. The woman was insatiable. She wanted more sex in more ways more often than anyone he'd ever met. "It's time to begin your training again."

"Yeah, okay," he croaked.

"Okay, *mistress*." She straddled him, glaring down, hands fisted on her hips, her onyx navel ring gleaming. *"Well?"*

His cock rose obediently, mighty and straight like that dude's sword, Excalibur.

Bodie grinned up at her. He was *the man*! "I'm ready, mistress."

"It's GOING TO be freezing!" Summer giggled nervously, holding Luke's hand, staring apprehensively at the water. They'd climbed down into the tiny cove behind her house after Luke got the completely insane idea that it would be fun to go swimming.

"It'll be awesome. We'll run, dive in, then turn around and run out. C'mon." He gave her arm a tug. "Ready? One, two—"

"No!" She pulled her hand away, unable to stop her nervous laughter. This was crazy. She couldn't believe he'd talked her into it. It was a nice evening, but the sun was on its way down, and the water temperature at this time of year was in the low fifties. Brr. Even putting a *toe* in would be painful.

Earlier this evening she and Luke had cooked a budget dinner of enchiladas at her house. He'd brought a six-pack of beer, and she'd had a couple that had gone straight to her head, because she rarely drank. Luke had also stopped at two cans, which pleased her. Didn't seem as if he had a problem there. Maybe that bar fight had been an isolated event. Stupid, but if controlling his alcohol intake wasn't a problem, there was hope the incident was safely in the past.

After dinner, she'd been ready to settle down with him in front of a movie, but Luke was determined to come out to swim—one of those ideas that sounded exciting and fun when she was warm in her own house, and entirely different when she was in a bathing suit facing the frigid water, about to go polar.

"C'mon, we'll run laps first to warm up." Luke started across the beach at an easy jog. She followed him to the other side by the cliffs, then back, then over again, then back, struggling to run on the soft sand, both of them giggling.

Summer had never, ever had this much fun with a guy. Maybe her younger brother when they were really little, before Ted had gotten into cigarettes, then pot, then drugs, and had changed into someone she no longer recognized.

She was crazy about Luke. When she was with him, she felt she could leave her baggage and burdens behind. But life wasn't just about fun, and she worried she was getting in too deep with someone who could just be killing time with her until he went back to his East Coast world, or until he "grew up," as he put it, and married someone more like himself. Even if he stayed around, she worried she'd leave him behind, still playing his way through life while she lived out her career dreams.

Summer shook off the concerns. Awfully heavy thoughts for a beautiful evening. They'd still be there the next day, and the next, though sooner or later she'd have to face them. Preferably before either she or Luke got hurt.

"One more!" Luke touched the cliff with her and they raced back to the other side, all of about twenty yards, their feet thumping on the sand. "Okay, you ready now?"

She was panting from their run. "I'll never...be ready. You're insane, you know that."

"I think I've heard that before, yeah." He was flushed, eyes sparking blue in the dimming light. "Never stopped me before, won't now. Come on."

He pulled her, laughing and protesting, down to the water's edge, where the sand hardened and became cold and wet under their toes.

"Stand here. Right here. Okay, on the count of three. Ready?"

"Luke! This is going to be horrible!"

"One..." He grabbed her hand. "Two...three!"

They ran, yelling and splashing into the icy waves until the water reached their waists, then they fell forward—it wasn't really diving—until they were submerged.

Argh! *Cold!*

Summer came up, gasping and shrieking, staggering to get out as quickly as possible. "That was enough swimming, even if it wasn't swimming. I'm outta here."

"Me, too. *Damn*, that's cold water."

"I told you." A wave pushed her forward. She fought for balance. No way was she going under again.

Luke lunged through the thigh-deep water to grab her arm, helping her the rest of the way onto the sand.

"Yes!" Luke thrust his arms overhead. "We did it! We were amazing!"

"We were morons!" She sprinted with him toward their beach towels, her skin tingling, lungs gasping for air.

"It was awesome!" Luke reached the towels first, unfolded one with a quick shake and draped it around her, using the edges to pull her close. "Admit it."

"Never!" She made the mistake of looking up at him. The setting sun cast a pink light over his face that made his skin rosy and his eyes stand out in strong relief. A lock of hair curled over his forehead, a drop of water sparkling at its tip. He'd put on weight since he'd been in California and had lost the starving-teenager look.

He was gorgeous. She really liked him. And she liked herself better since meeting him. He'd gotten her out of her rut and reminded her that life could hold joy and silliness as well as work and responsibility.

"Summer."

"Yes." Her voice came out husky, the way a woman speaks when she's overcome with nerves and emotion. She did not want her resolve to stay platonic with Luke tested right now. She was too vulnerable, he was too handsome, the beach too romantic.

"I, uh—" He cleared his throat. "I want to tell you that I think you're really beautiful."

"Thanks." She felt herself blush, dropping her eyes, unable to look into his anymore. "You're pretty hot yourself."

"Yeah?" She could hear the pleasure in his voice. "So does that mean we can do it? Right now? On the beach? Without protection? I hear girls don't get pregnant the first time if they—"

Summer let out a howl of pretend horror. A pretty convincing one.

"I'm *kidding*." He was laughing. "Jeez, Summer, you think I'm *that* clueless?"

"Yes." She folded her arms over her chest and glared at him, trying not to laugh. "You're a guy."

"You should have seen your face."

"Not *fun*-ny."

"I thought you were going to have a total—"

One push was all it took when he was off balance like that. Then he was getting sandy everywhere and Summer was standing triumphantly over him. "Ha! And I knew you were kidding, temper boy."

"Yeah?" He lay there, grinning up at her. "I'm glad to hear that, uptight girl."

"You're going to have to rinse off that sand."

"So are you."

Summer frowned. "I'm not sandy."

He hooked his leg behind hers and brought her down to sprawl over his hard chest, locking her there in his strong arms. "Now you are."

"You are so going to pay for that." She struggled up on her arms and tried to glare at him some more, but he looked so pleased with himself that she couldn't help laughing.

Then he pulled her back down onto his wet, warm torso and kissed her. His kisses were salty and sandy and sweet, the most wonderful kisses she'd ever had.

Her instinct should have been to pull away. She knew what happened when guys kissed you and there was nothing between you but bathing suits. Sooner or later, the sweetness would evaporate from the kiss, the tongue would come out and the groping would start.

But she really, really liked kissing Luke.

He smiled at her, lifting his hand to brush sand from her cheek. "You okay?"

"Yes." She wasn't sure. She felt fragile and shimmering, not very much like her solid, serious self.

Luke helped her to her feet, still loose limbed and relaxed. "I didn't plan to do that. It just sorta happened. You looked so pretty, and I don't know, I just wanted to."

"Okay." She didn't know what else to say. She should tell him it wasn't going to happen again until they'd figured out a lot more about each other, but with the warmth of his mouth so recently against her lips…

"So, hey, guess what, Summer Kreuger?" He raised his eyebrows, apparently not remotely as affected by kissing her as she'd been by kissing him. A good thing to keep in mind if she ever got weak-kneed around him again.

"What, Luke Arnette?" She imitated his careless tone.

"I got a job today."

"What? Oh, wow!" Summer clapped her hands together. "Luke, that's fantastic. Why did you wait so long to tell me?"

He tipped his head, eyeing her sheepishly. "I don't know. It's not that impressive."

"It's great. Where are you working?"

"Bagel shop in San Luis Obispo."

"It's fine for now. Are you going back to school?"

"Oh…maybe. Hey, you're shivering. Let's go back and get you warmed up." He picked up the towel, shook it free of sand and draped it back over her shoulders.

Summer's balloon of optimism popped. *Maybe* wasn't exactly an enthusiastic response. In fact, she'd bet it was a euphemism for *probably not*. She shouldn't be disappointed. They were just friends, right? Or…friends who kissed sometimes…she still wasn't sure what that had been about. Maybe it was as simple as he'd said—him kissing a girl because he thought she looked pretty and he wanted to. A reflex, like petting a dog or cooing over a baby.

In any case, Luke's plans for his life shouldn't matter so much to her.

She'd just have to try to forget that they already did.

THIS VALENTINE'S THING was going to kill her. Chris hung up the phone in the Slow Pour office, her eyes practically crossing from fatigue. Everything was in place, the food on order, the entertainment, the prizes, the red carpet for kneeling all taken care of, but after the phone call from Eva on Monday night, she had about as much enthusiasm for a day devoted to love as a woman whose hopes for romance had recently swirled down the potty of circumstances.

Fact one: she could not commit to any kind of extended relationship with Zac right now, no matter how serious her feelings seemed, because early infatuation wasn't to be trusted.

Fact two: she needed time to see if those feelings were the real thing or not.

Fact three: since Eva and Ames were moving back here to California and she was moving back to New York, she did not have time.

Fact four: see facts one and two, on and on into infinity.

And that was that. Well thought-out. Smart. And infallibly sensible.

But well thought-out, smart and sensible were making her feel horrible. Obviously what she really wanted was to continue a relationship with Zac. She had to keep reasoning with herself that while her feelings for Zac might be real, a long-distance relationship wasn't a reliable test of compatibility. When you were apart, the longing for the other person was exaggerated, and when you were together, it was always a honeymoon period of reunion followed by the intense emotions stemming from having to part again so soon.

Sorry, inner voice, her common sense was right this time. No matter how strongly she felt about Zac, trying to keep a relationship going was not the best course. Right now the best course was to take back to New York all she'd learned about herself while she was here. She had new insights into her less desirable behaviors and, having met Zac, a higher bar of how she wanted to be treated in relationships in the future, and a better idea of how she wanted to treat her next partner. Once there, she'd be starting over in a way—she'd call it the New Chris, but by now that concept made her want to hurl.

Moving back to New York was going to be exciting. She'd be a better and stronger woman taking on the city, one block at a time. Or something like that.

Yeah, she could barely hold back from jumping up and down.

No, no, it would take time, but she'd have time. Nothing but time. And Zac was a really special guy. She was sure they'd be able to remain friends.

Whoopee.

Sick of arguing with herself, Chris took a deep breath to try to release the constant knot of pain in her chest and went over the list for the next day's event one more time, making sure everything was under control and ready to go. The last customer of the evening was packing up to leave. Eva and Summer would be over soon to help decorate the shop. Then she was going to go over to see Zac and explain everything she'd finally gotten straight in her mind.

She'd live through this.

Back behind the counter, she was relieved to see the guy who'd been at the same table most of the day playing video games over cup after cup of espresso was gone—probably to spend the night wide-awake playing more video games—which meant she could turn the sign to Closed and start bringing out the decorations.

She'd just finished stacking boxes by the order-pickup area when Eva appeared at the front door, apparently already dressed for the holiday in pink pants and a white top with red hearts.

Chris let her in. "Wow, look at you. What will you have left to wear tomorrow?"

"I'll surprise you. Hi, sweetie." Eva gave her sister a long hug, then pulled back and searched Chris's face. "How are you doing?"

Chris felt an unfair jolt of irritation at her twin's concern, and was instantly ashamed. Eva and Ames were living their lives the way they should be. The fact that everything was coming up roses for them while Chris wallowed in weeds, well, that was just the way it was right now. She couldn't blame her sister. "I'm okay."

"Yeah?" Eva studied her through narrowed eyes. "You look awful."

"I am awful, thank you." She shrugged, knowing better than to lie, and handed Eva the box of bright red centerpieces—small red vases holding bouquets of reflective metallic red strands decorated with hearts. "But I'll get over it. And him. Here. One of those goes on each table."

"Get over Zac?" Eva clutched the box, staring at Chris over the top. "Why do you have to get over him? I thought everything was going great. Except for the whole moving-back-to-New-York part."

"Yeah, and there goes our chance for a relationship." She moved back to the stack of boxes to retrieve the one containing garlands of red and pink hearts.

Eva followed her, still holding her box. "Wait, why? What if he gets into Columbia?"

"He doesn't hear for weeks, so we can't plan on that." She carried the garland box over toward the register, Eva trailing her. "And I'm too old to be pining after some guy who lives two thousand miles away."

She thumped the box on the counter, bracing herself for the slew of unreasonable arguments Eva would come up with. Maybe one of them could convince her she was wrong. That would be nice.

"I understand. I really do. I was exactly where you are, remember? You and I were supposed to switch back at the end of October, and Ames had a really good job in New York. I was so crazy about him, and I had no idea what to do."

"I remember. But then I decided to stay here longer, and you lucked out that Ames was able to relocate." Chris took Eva's arm and steered her back to a table, removing the box from her arms. "One centerpiece per table."

"I did luck out." Eva followed Chris back to the counter. "But we would have worked something out regardless. He was incredibly special to me from the beginning, different from every guy I'd ever dated, and I would have been miserable without him."

"I'm sure I will be, too, at first. But there's someone in New York for me, I'm sure." Chris pointed Eva firmly back to the centerpieces. "One for each table?"

"He won't be like Zac."

Kaboom. Five little words, and every fear Chris had been battling back into the swamps clambered out, smelly and dripping.

"We'll see." She barely managed to get the words out.

"Hi, sorry I'm late." Summer pushed through the front

door. "Luke dropped me off. He makes me late for everything."

Eva looked up from ripping open her box. "Because he can't manage his time or because you can't bear to leave him?"

"Yes." Summer was beaming.

Chris was so happy for her. And she also wanted to ask Summer please not to look that joyful again until Chris was safely back in New York.

"So besides the fact that you can't tear yourself away from him…" Eva put a centerpiece on one of the tables—not in the center. "Are we talking romance yet or still just friendship?"

Summer hesitated. "We're friends. It seems to work best that way."

"How come?"

"Eva." Chris rolled her eyes, taping a length of garland to the counter. "Let the woman have some privacy. Summer, I've got honeycomb heart thingies for you to hang from the ceiling. There are hooks already up there."

"Oh, yes!" Eva pointed them out delightedly. "Those are from when we had the first-anniversary party for the store, remember, Summer? We hung little boxes wrapped to look like presents. Gosh, it will be so good to come back."

Chris clung to the box of honeycomb heart decorations, not trusting herself to speak. She could not believe she was being such a crybaby about this.

Hey. She was allowed. This was hard.

"Thanks, Chris." Summer took the box and headed for the ladder.

"Sorry for prying." Eva put down another noncentered centerpiece. "I just want to see you happy. You've had it rough."

"We'll see what happens." She dragged the ladder under one of the ceiling hooks. "I'm not sure we're right for each other."

"Really?" Eva said. "Why not?"

Summer looked cornered, as people often did when Eva got going with her questions. "We come from different worlds."

"I'm sure he doesn't care."

"Maybe not now…" Summer climbed the ladder and hung the first honeycomb heart from the ceiling.

"Wait, wait, let me get this straight." Eva approached the ladder, having abandoned the centerpieces once again. Chris took quick advantage, quietly moving through the room, placing each in the exact middle of the table. "You're not going to give Luke a chance because it might not work out?"

Summer scrunched up her face in confusion. She looked adorable. "Well, don't put it like *that*."

Eva shoved her hands on her hips. "I'm telling you, these Arnettes are good guys, one in a million. Okay, I don't know Luke, but be glad he's nothing like your previous boyfriends, Summer. They deserved eternal torment as far as I'm concerned."

"Can you arrange that?" She dragged the ladder over to the next hook. "Luke is a good guy. But he's a floater. One thing, then the other. Nothing taken too seriously. Nothing lasts too long. I don't want to be hurt by that."

"I don't blame you." Chris taped another length of garland and crossed her eyes at Eva's glare.

"Well, I do. This is a kid who had a serious tragedy early in his life, and a pretty crappy childhood, from what Zac's told me, who messed up once and has been paying for it ever since. He had to give up his school, his friends, his part of the country. No wonder he doesn't want to commit to anything right now."

Summer froze on the ladder, blinking down at Eva.

"And you." Eva whirled on Chris. "You were incredibly brittle when you came out here, exhausted and beaten down. Once you settled in, you immediately started sounding like your old self again, maybe even coming out of your usual shell a little. Then you go through this weird Peace, Love and Coma thing and start sounding like you're half-dead."

Chris narrowed her eyes. "Hey, I was—"

"And now, these last couple of weeks, you've been sounding wonderful and excited and free, Chris. Different than I've ever seen you." Eva pointed emphatically. "So, the big question is, for one million dollars, Chris Meyer, guess who was part of your life both times you were feeling better than you ever have in your life?"

Chris froze at the counter, blinking at Eva.

"I rest my case." She clapped her hands together.

They finished decorating, Chris and Summer mostly in stunned silence, Eva chatty and self-satisfied.

Was she right? Had Chris really come alive when Zac was around? Did that mean her big transformations had less to do with the Peace, Love and Joy Center or California and more to do with Zac?

It was possible. It made sense. It changed nothing.

They worked on until the store was Valentined up the wazoo, then they put away the boxes and the ladder. Summer and Chris emerged from the office to find Eva holding a bottle of champagne and three plastic cups.

"Now that's done and looking fabulous, we are going to polish off this entire bottle of champagne, because we are celebrating." She separated the cups and put them onto a table.

"What are we celebrating?" Chris exchanged what-the-heck glances with Summer and the two women walked over to Eva. "Ames's job?"

"That, sure." She eased out the cork, which emitted a satisfying *thwunk*.

"Your move back to Slow Pour?" Summer asked.

"That, sure." Eva poured a glass and handed it to her.

"You and Ames getting married someday?"

"That, sure." Eva handed Chris a glass and poured one for herself. "But mostly…"

"Your pregnancy?" Chris asked sweetly.

"Ack! No way." Eva glared at her, then raised her glass up high and waited for them to do the same, looking slyly back and forth between them. "We are celebrating today, because some time tomorrow, outside this very shop, *someone* will be getting engaged."

Chris and Summer looked at each other, then back at Eva. *"Who?"*

14

"I'M DONE. I'M going in." Luke struggled to his feet amid tumbling foam from yet another wipeout, his soaked hair sticking out in all directions, and retrieved his surfboard—one of Zac's old ones. "No offense, but this sport is ridiculous."

"You did fine." Zac paddled toward him, letting a small wave speed him along. He was also ready to come in, though the breaks were good that morning, and not crowded. He'd thought spending some time out in the water and out of his head might make him feel better. Usually it did. Today, not so much. "It takes a while to get the feel of it."

"Yeah, well, I need about a year to recover my ego and dignity before I try again."

"You should have seen me the first time." Zac stood and picked up his board. "Leg tangled in the leash, board bonking me on the head. It was ugly."

"If you say so." Luke walked alongside him, stumbling and swearing when an unexpected wave caught him behind the knees. "I'm not sure how much seawater you have to drink before you die, but I've got to be close."

"I'll take you to the hospital when you're critical."

"Wow. Thanks." Luke headed for their towels and practically threw the board onto the sand.

Zac placed his board gently next to his brother's and picked up a towel to dry his face. "What's going on, Luke?"

"What do you mean?"

"You're in a crappy mood. How come?"

Luke imitated his stance, legs parted, hands on his hips, and met Zac's challenging stare with one of his own. "What's going on, Zac? You're in a crappy mood, too. How come?"

Zac pressed his lips together. Did twenty-one-year-olds hold some contest every year to see who could have the pissiest attitude? It was on the tip of his tongue to say, *I asked you first*, but he was supposed to be the mature one.

"Because it's really early in the morning on Valentine's Day and I'm with you."

Luke's glare faltered. "I thought things were going really well with Chris. Didn't you go out last night?"

"Yup."

"So what happened, she dump you?"

"We weren't really dating, just…" He stopped, out of years of habit of protecting his brother, before he reminded himself Luke was plenty old enough for the concept of casual sex.

"What?" Luke narrowed his eyes incredulously. "What are you talking about? You're crazy about her. This wasn't just hooking up."

"For her it was."

"No." Luke shook his head emphatically. "It wasn't. Summer told me she's sure that—"

"Yeah, Jackie told me, too. But if it's not Chris telling

me, it doesn't make any difference. And last night she told me it was over."

Luke frowned, picked up the other towel and scrubbed it over his hair and face. "That makes no sense."

"She has to move back to New York. Maybe she's just protecting herself. And me. There's nothing I can do."

Luke threw his towel down. "Zac, man, listen to yourself. You're doing it again. What can I do about it? Nothing. How much testosterone do I have left? None!'"

"What *should* I do, Luke? Tell her I've decided she can't go back to New York? Tell her she has to stay in a relationship with me even though she doesn't want one?" He stalked over to his board. "Come on, let's go back to the car."

"Dude, I'm sorry." Luke went to get his board. "I know that really sucks."

"I'll be fine." He wasn't so sure. It felt as if a knife thrower was practicing with his heart as the target.

"Did you tell her how you felt?"

Zac glared at him. "Who made you my therapist?"

"Did you tell her you love her?"

"She doesn't want to *be* with me, Luke. What good will that do? I might as well cut off my balls and have them gift wrapped."

Luke cringed. "*Oh*, bad image, bro."

"Give me a year off to save my ego and my dignity."

"Okay, okay." Luke held up his hands. "I hear you. I get it."

They trudged up the steep hillside path toward Zac's car. It was overcast and the air was cool but thick with humidity, which didn't help Zac's mood. But he might as well face it—nothing was going to help his mood. Including being a jerk to his brother.

"Sorry, Luke," he mumbled.

"Whatever. Today sucks. End of story."

"Yeah? What's going on with you?"

"Summer." He adjusted his hold on the board. "She's not that into me, either."

Zac laughed bitterly. "This was all so much easier in grade school, wasn't it."

"Yeah." Luke snorted. "Remember that girl from boarding school who had the crush on you, Sylvia or something?"

"You remember that?" Zac turned in amazement. "You were barely in kindergarten."

"Dad told me about her. He said she called you every day until he told her to get lost."

"Uh-huh." Zac smiled wryly, putting his board down next to the car. "He told her *nice* girls don't chase after guys."

"Like you were only *nice* if you stayed home hoping the phone would ring."

"I don't know, maybe it was easier when everyone knew what to expect." Zac hoisted his board onto the Prius's roof rack. "Boys did the chasing, girls got chased."

"Elephant seals still do it that way." Luke put his board on top of Zac's and flashed a smile at his brother's expression. "Summer took me to the rookery."

"That's a cool place." He retrieved the straps to tie down the boards from the back of the car. "So what's going on with her?"

"She's too good for me."

"Hey, *I* could have told you that." He fastened the strap to one side of the rack, grinning to show he was teasing. "What makes you think so?"

"She's got her life all figured out. College, graduate school, career."

"Summer?" He was surprised, and then he wasn't. Not

at all. She was smart, a hard worker and a great listener with a good heart. "Good for her."

"I don't think she's that into dating a dropout who sells bagels."

Zac threw him a look. "So get a life, dude."

"I *have* a life."

"Selling bagels."

"That's a life if it's what you want to do."

"I agree." Zac tossed the strap across the top of the surfboards for Luke to secure the other side. "But I don't think it's what you want to do."

Luke sighed. Sounded as if Zac had scored a point there. "Maybe not. Thing is, you know, she wants to do all this stuff and she has no money. I have no ambition but tons of money. I wish there was some way I could help her."

Zac secured the second strap. "Marry her and pay her tuition."

"Yeah, right." Luke burst out laughing. Harder than the joke warranted. Much harder. Almost maniacally. "Yeah, *right*."

"You've thought about it." Zac stared at him, frozen in the act of throwing the second strap over. "You're in love with her."

Luke stopped laughing. His face flushed. He looked slightly sick. "I think I might be."

"Yeah, well, there's this thing about love." Zac threw over the second strap, then walked around the car, since Luke showed no signs of being helpful. "You aren't one hundred percent invested in what you want anymore. It becomes at least half about the other person."

"Yeah. That's how it feels." Luke stepped back. "I dunno, maybe I'm growing up."

"You decide what's best for you, and what's best for her. If you're lucky, they turn out to be the same thing."

Luke ran his finger back and forth along the top of the car window, then his face suddenly cleared.

"You know? I'm not sure how you stumbled onto that, but it actually might make sense." Luke punched Zac on the shoulder, beaming, the age-old guy method of avoiding a hug. "And now let me teach *you* something about love, big brother."

"Oh, no." Zac rolled his eyes, yanking the strap tight. "Here it comes. Go ahead."

"You see…" Luke put his arm around Zac's shoulders and gestured grandly into the air. "Love is like a tree falling in a forest with no one around."

"Uh-huh." Zac rolled his eyes. "How does that work?"

"Funny you should ask. I was just going to tell you."

"Luke…"

"If Chris doesn't hear that you're in love with her, dude, then as far as she's concerned, you're not."

SUMMER SAT ON Zac's front stoop, clutching a Slow Pour bag containing assorted muffins, Suja juices and coffee, feeling stupid. Coming here this morning to bring Luke breakfast on Valentine's Day had seemed like a great idea. She didn't have to work until one—Chris's event started at three—so she and Luke could have breakfast and hang out, the way they'd done the day they went to see the elephant seals.

One problem: it had never occurred to her that Luke might not be home. She'd taken it for granted that at 9:00 a.m. on a Saturday he'd still be asleep. Zac hadn't answered the door, either, and Luke wasn't answering his phone. He wasn't supposed to start his new job until Monday, so that couldn't be it…

Since Eva had made her comments last night, Summer had been thinking a lot about Luke. About how even she had sensed that for all his outer cockiness, inside, Luke was shaken and unsure. Still, she'd lumped him into the trouble category along with her previous disastrous relationships, had made assumptions based on assumptions and then used those to talk herself out of her feelings for him.

After spending too many hours awake, she'd finally decided she owed it to him to start over in her approach, to stop making assumptions and really listen to what he had to say.

Luke deserved that. But where the hell was he, because she was anxious to talk things out with him and see how he reacted, try to figure out what his real feelings were for her. Maybe he'd go back to school someday, maybe he wouldn't, but she couldn't penalize him for not being there now.

And speaking of where he was, why wasn't he home?

She was nearly ready to give up when Zac's blue car rounded the corner with two surfboards mounted on top. Had Zac and Luke been surfing? She didn't think Luke knew how. Or had Zac gone with someone else?

"Hey, Summer!" A dark head popped out of the passenger-side window. It was Luke and he was grinning at her. Summer's heart jumped and her mouth spread in an answering smile. She'd never been that happy to see anyone in her life.

Clearly it had been a waste of time to fight falling for him. She'd fallen so hard she'd landed flat on her face.

"What are you doing here?" He jumped out of the car and strode up the front walk, his hair wet.

"Were you catching some waves this morning?"

"Nah. I don't know how to surf." He rolled his eyes

sheepishly. "I did, however, spend a lot of time wiping out."

"Sounds about right for a first time."

"What is that?" He pointed to the Slow Pour bag.

"Breakfast." She lifted it. "And an apology."

"That sounds strangely familiar." He squatted in front of her, searching her face. "But I have no idea what you'd want to apologize for."

She focused over his shoulder on Zac, who'd locked the car and was coming toward them, looking about as miserable as Chris had the night before. It was Valentine's Day morning; he and Chris should be together.

"Hey, Summer."

"Hi, Zac. How were the waves this morning?"

"Not bad. I figured if Luke here wants to be a California boy he's got to learn, so I dragged him out of bed."

"Yeah, I think I'm fine being from Connecticut, thanks."

"Aw, you'll learn." Zac glanced at Summer, then at the Slow Pour bag in her lap, then at his watch. "You know, I have some errands to do. I think I'll just unload the boards and go. Should take me at least a couple of hours."

Summer grinned up at him; he winked and strode back to the car.

Zac was the best.

"Want to come inside?" Luke stood and held out a hand to help her up. "I'm going to shower quick and get into some warmer clothes."

"Sure." She could have cheered. Her plan was working out perfectly.

While Luke showered, she roamed Zac's kitchen, finding plates, napkins and most important—a vase. She'd just put the finishing touches on the table when Luke reappeared, wearing a long-sleeved shirt and jeans, his hair still wet but combed now. He'd gotten a little sun at the beach, and the fresh color in his face brought out the vivid blue of his eyes even more strongly.

"Hey, what's this?"

Summer gestured proudly to the flowers, two white tulips and two purple hyacinths. "I couldn't afford as many as I wanted to get you."

"Summer, you shouldn't have done this for me." He came to stand next to her, smelling of spicy soap and shampoo. She wanted to taste him. "You're saving your money."

"I know, but—" Summer shrugged "—this was important."

"This was incredibly sweet." He put his hands on her shoulders and turned her toward him. "Now apologize for whatever you think you did so I can forgive you, because I'm starving. And then we have other stuff to talk about, too."

"Okay." She made herself look at him while she spoke, though it would've been much easier to apologize to the floor. "I'm sorry that I haven't been more understanding about what you've been through. I'm sorry that I keep pushing college on you. The truth is…"

Deep breath. This was the hard part.

"I have come to— That is, I have started— The reason I've been—" She let out an exasperated growl and decided talking to the floor would be just fine. "I kept wanting you to be the guy I've always fantasized about. In so many ways you are. But it's not fair to expect you to become something that's important only to me, and not to you. So I'm sorry."

She peeked up to see his reaction. He looked stunned, and not necessarily in a good way. Her heart sank. Had she blown it? At least she'd finally been honest, with herself and with him. That was more important than what happened next, right?

Maybe. She hoped so.

"Are you saying that I'm not your ultimate fantasy?" He clutched his chest. "I can't *believe* it."

"Luke." She put her hands on her hips. For probably the hundredth time since she'd known him, she was outraged and also about to burst out laughing. "That was really hard to do, and now you're making fun of me?"

"Of course I am." He took her into his arms. She resisted firmly—for about one thousandth of a second. "It's just what I do."

"Humph."

"Thank you for your apology, but it was completely unnecessary. All you've done as far as I'm concerned is remind me that the world was not put here for my amusement. And I want you to know that I know that. In fact, I've been doing a lot of thinking."

"Ooh, gosh, that must hurt."

He gave her the look she deserved. "Here's what I'm thinking. You and Zac are both going to school in the fall. After my grades at UConn the last semester, I have no idea what kind of place would take me, but by then I'll be ready to try."

Summer smiled so wide her mouth hurt, and it still didn't feel wide enough. "Oh, Luke, that's wonderful. As long as it's really what you want."

"It is. But wait, there's more. With Zac gone, that means there will be an empty bedroom here. It makes no sense for you to be sleeping in a living room. If you and I are still able to stand each other in September, I think you should live here, rent-free."

She gaped at him, her mind spinning. Part of her wanted to jump at the chance to save that much money;

the other was immediately rejecting the idea of accepting charity. "Luke, you can't—"

"Actually, I can. And Zac thinks it's a great idea, too."

She stared at him, bewildered by the depth of his generosity to a woman he considered just a friend.

And then her brain came up with another possibility.

"Are you asking me to move in with you?"

"Yes. Either as friends. Or..." He took in a long breath. "The truth is, I want to be the guy you've always fantasized about. Because you're that for me."

Giddy with joy, somehow Summer managed to make herself look horrified. "Your fantasy is that I'm a *guy*?"

"Summer." He faked outrage, tightening his arms around her. "That was really hard to do, and now you're making fun of me?"

"Of course I am." She reached up on tiptoe to kiss him, and the kisses were as warm and wonderful and sweet as she remembered, only this time there was no fear that Luke Arnette would be trouble. Deep down in her soul she sensed that he was the man for her. Forever.

"It's just what I do."

15

THE VALENTINE'S DAY event at Slow Pour was turning out to be a smash. Almost. The morning's cloudy skies had cleared to brilliant blue. The tent outside was crowded, and people even spilled onto the sidewalk, sipping coffee and eating pastries, trusting that if any proposals happened they'd be able to see.

Two local papers were there, and a *USA Today* reporter, in the area for a story on Central Coast wines, had stopped by to check out the scene and have a tall latte with a heart-shaped peanut-butter brownie. Four photographers and hundreds of cell phones were at the ready. The red carpet stood empty in the middle of the tent, where Chris had laid it that morning.

All they needed was the first proposal.

It was early yet—the event had only been on for an hour, and they had two more to go. She wasn't panicking.

Zac wasn't there. She hadn't really expected him to be. Their talk late last night had been really hard on both of them, but Chris still felt strongly that she'd made the right decision. Every time she wavered, she remembered what he'd said on the drive up to Jackie's friend's house—

if he had serious feelings about a woman, nothing would stop him from trying for forever.

Apparently she'd stopped him.

"Hey, Chris." Eva tapped her on the shoulder. Today she had on red leggings and red ankle boots with a pink shirt covered in red-and-white polka dots. Heart-shaped pins held up her wavy blond hair. Trust Eva to have more than one outfit suitable for Valentine's Day. "Jinx said the event at NYEspresso is going really well. The pastry-chef thing got great buzz and people are flocking to the café. I admit, I'm glad I'm here, though. This is totally exciting."

"Any chance you can get Ames to propose and start things off?"

She snorted. "*That's* not going to happen. Totally not his style to make it a public event. But you're right, it would be perfect. Getting engaged at my own shop? I'd love that."

Her shop. Ames was starting his new job two weeks from Monday. Eva was flying back to New York tomorrow to pack up her stuff and help Ames pack his, and then she was coming back for good. She wanted to put her house in Carmia on the market and start looking for a place for the two of them right away.

Chris would have to start packing soon.

The crowd noise swelled into a roar of approval. Chris craned her neck toward the center of the tent. Was someone proposing?

Yes!

"Eva." She grabbed her twin's arm. "Man on the carpet! Come on, let's go."

Eva squealed with excitement. "Awesome! You've done it!"

They pushed their way to a spot with a good view,

since she and Eva would be in charge of handing out the free coffee certificates. The beaming couple in the center of the carpet was instantly familiar.

"Gus and Pammy!" Chris thumped a hand to her chest. "Oh, my gosh!"

"Already? You have got to be kidding me." Eva's voice sounded in her ear. "Didn't they just meet?"

Chris nodded, totally enchanted. Gus was on both knees, hands clasped over Pammy's, his eyes glowing with love. The crowd quieted.

"Pammy, you are the sunshine of my life. You give me hope to carry on. You are the wind beneath my waves. I love you. Will you marry me?"

"Oh, yes, Gus. Oh, my gosh, yes." Pammy had her hands to her face, tears sliding over her fingers.

"All right!" Gus got to his feet, pulled her up and dipped her, kissing her as if it was the last thing he'd be allowed to do on earth. Cameras and flashes went off all around. The crowd erupted into cheers.

Chris clapped and yelled along with everyone else, brushing away her own tears. The way Gus had looked at Pammy… Oh, boy.

She'd better give them the certificates right away or she was going to start sobbing.

Stepping onto the carpet, she held up her hand for the crowd to quiet down. "Gus and Pammy, congratulations! Eva and I and all the staff at Slow Pour wish you a long and happy marriage. This certificate is good for one free coffee for each of you every day for a year."

The crowd applauded again. Chris hugged Pammy and then Gus, who picked her up off the ground and swung her around until she feared she was going to lose her lunch.

"Thanks, Chris." He put her down, looking so happy

and so handsome she got choked up all over again. "Neither of us drinks coffee. I just really wanted to ask Pammy to marry me."

"How about a year of free Suja Juice?"

"Whoa!" He nodded and raised his hand for a high five. "Excellent."

Chris grinned and gave his hand a resounding smack. "You go, dude."

"By the way, Bodie called me finally. He's fine. He said he just got tied up. I think I'll—"

"Gus!" Eva launched herself at him. "Congratulations!"

"Thanks, coffee lady."

Eva congratulated Pammy, then the happy couple made their way into the crowd to accept backslaps and high fives from friends and strangers alike.

Chris stood watching them, giving in to a shuddering sigh and a little sniff.

Eva gave her a strange look. "Since when have you been such a romantic?"

"Me?" She shrugged. *Since I met Zac.* "I don't know. I'm just emotional these days."

"Uh-huh." Eva nodded sagely, tapping her finger on her chin. "Do we know why?"

"Yeah, we do." She gave her twin a sad smile.

"And what does that tell you about—"

"Hey, ladies." Ames joined them, looking handsome in a crisp blue shirt and khakis. He slipped his arm around Eva, who lit up like a Christmas tree. "Wasn't that great? You got one."

"It was fabulous. I hope they make it." Eva put her arm around Ames and gave him a squeeze. Her face changed. "Ow. What is that? You have something sharp in your pocket."

"Oh, yeah?" He winked at Chris, who smiled politely, having no idea what was cute and mysterious about jabbing your girlfriend. "What do you think that's about?"

"*I* don't know. It's *your* pocket." Eva moved away and swatted at a square bulge in his pants.

"Let me see." He rummaged around, then with a flourish, pulled out a black velvet box. "Oh, hey, yeah, I wondered where that went."

Eva gasped. "Ames!"

"Man on the carpet!" Chris could barely get the words out. Her sister was about to get engaged! She was bursting with happiness.

Ames knelt. Eva immediately sank down with him and they joined hands, gazing rapturously at each other. A soft *ooh* spread over the crowd before it quieted into electric anticipation.

"Eva, you have brought so much joy and laughter to my life."

"You know we already get free coffee?" Eva's eyes were sparking equal parts mischief and joy.

"Wait, really? Jeez, what am I doing here?" The crowd laughed. Ames waited, gazing at Eva, who was gazing back at him, their expressions so full of love that Chris started bawling again. They were going to be happy forever. She wasn't going to be able to take much more of this. At least she'd been smart enough to wear waterproof mascara.

Gradually the crowd settled again.

"Eva Meyer, love of my life, will you marry me?"

"Yes, yes and yes, Ames Cooke. I can't think of anything I'd rather do."

More cheers, more excitement, more clicking cameras aimed at the kissing couple.

"Hey, Chris, are you okay?" A slender arm enveloped Chris in a fierce hug.

"Aw, Summer, thanks." Chris wiped her tears, glad to see Luke standing next to Summer. The two of them looked happy and right together. "This is really perfect. And a bit brutal."

"I know, it really must be. But you've done so much for Slow Pour today and for Carmia, too. We're going to miss you. *I'm* going to miss you."

"No, stop!" Chris was half laughing, half crying. "Please, have mercy on the tear ducts."

"It's going great." Luke nodded, smiling crookedly. "I'm sorry I couldn't get Zac to come by. He said he had stuff to do."

"Oh." She nodded. "I understand."

All too well. He didn't want to see her. And with her emotions set on ultraturmoil right now, she didn't think she could handle seeing him, either. She wasn't even sure she could make it through the rest of this event.

She did. By the time darkness fell, two more proposals had been made and accepted, and finally the last of the stragglers had gone home. Chris had sent Ames and Eva off to celebrate. Ames's plans included a fancy dinner in San Luis Obispo and spending the night at an incredible resort hotel on a cliff overlooking the ocean.

Chris, Summer and Luke had cleaned up and put away everything but the tent and the red carpet. The rental company would come pick up the tent on Monday. The red carpet Chris had decided to leave as a temporary tribute to the four couples who had committed to each other here today. When word got around she expected people who had missed the event would come by to gawk.

"Thanks, guys. Go home. You've been fabulous. I'm going to do one last check inside."

"Okay." Summer hugged her long and hard. "Luke and I are going to hang out at my house, make dinner and watch TV. You're welcome to come over."

Chris smiled. *Oh, Lord.* The offer was incredibly sweet, but it meant she'd become the single woman everyone felt sorry for. "Thanks, but I'm exhausted. I'll be fine at home."

Eva's home. Chris's home was thousands of miles away, and she suddenly missed it something fierce.

Almost as much as she missed Zac.

"If you're sure." Summer hugged her again. "If you change your mind, just call. Seriously, we'll just be hanging out."

"Thanks, Summer." The back of Chris's head was aching from forcing so many smiles. She just wanted to curl up alone on the couch and cry herself into puffy-faced hideousness. Then, phoenix from the ashes, she'd rise up again and be okay.

That was the plan, anyway.

After Summer and Luke left, she went back into Slow Pour for her purse, lingering by the table where she'd first met Zac back in October, and had been both strongly attracted and strongly annoyed by everything he did. He'd practically bullied her into taking a walk to the beach that day, showing her the special peaceful place on the cliff where she'd been so many times since to meditate. From that first meeting he'd seen what she needed and tried to give it to her.

To repay him, she'd fought or denied her true feelings, bristled whenever he spoke to her, and once she started to understand and change, she'd given all the credit to herself and the Peace, Love and Joy Center.

She owed him so much. Before she left, she'd make

sure to speak with him and let him know how much his support had meant to her.

How much *he* meant to her?

Chris closed her eyes. She wasn't going there. What was the point?

She opened the office, got out her purse and did the final check on the store before turning the sign to Closed and locking up. Outside, she wandered over to the tent, dimly lit by nearby streetlights. The red carpet beckoned her. She stood next to it, reliving the special, intimate moments the four couples had shared with Slow Pour and with Carmia.

The deep ache in her chest intensified. She lowered her head, feeling tears coming again. Again! This was getting to be a habit, and would continue, she suspected, until she was back home once again and could immerse herself in the crazy hustle of New York and her business.

"Chris."

Her head jerked up and her heart took off. *Zac.*

He ducked under the roof flap of the tent and walked toward her, stopping on the other side of the carpet, hands on his hips, looking big and solid and absolutely wonderful. "I'm sorry I missed your event."

"Oh, that's…" She had to clear her throat. "That's okay. It was great, though. Four couples got engaged."

"Yeah, Luke texted me. He told me about Eva and Ames. And Gus. That's great." He nodded. Nodded again.

Oh, Zac. Chris felt as if she was going to explode from all the feelings fighting inside her.

A sudden breeze blew through the tent, bringing the cool, damp smell of incoming fog. Apparently the clear skies weren't going to last much longer.

"I wanted to talk to you, Chris." He was calm, as usual, watching her intently. She'd come to love both of those things about him. "I figured if I showed up earlier you'd be a little busy."

"Just a bit." She wrapped her arms around herself, bracing for another draining conversation.

"In all the time we've been together, you've been searching for ways to be as emotionally honest with yourself as possible." His voice cracked. "But I haven't been emotionally honest with you."

"Oh." Her head sagged back down toward her chest. *No more, no more.* No more emotions today. No more complications. She felt as fragile and doomed as a soap bubble heading for a rosebush.

Pop. The end.

Zac's feet took a step forward, to the edge of the carpet.

"Zac…"

"I love you."

Chris's head rose. Her eyes widened. Her lips parted. Had she just heard him say what she'd just heard him say?

He was looking at her tenderly, his blue eyes warm, his face solemn and incredibly sweet. "I love you, Chris. I've known for a long time. I should have told you before."

She needed to say something. But what? How would this change anything? What if she—

Shut up, Chris.

"I love you, too, Zac."

It was so simple.

The second the words were out of her mouth, she felt as if ten tons of misery lifted off her shoulders and shot straight up and exploded into fireworks, lighting the sky with stars of blazing color.

Yes, she was getting the hang of this romantic thing.

It took about half a second for her and Zac to cross the carpet and find each other in the middle. A fraction of that time for their arms to encircle one another, for their mouths to meet.

The fireworks were still exploding, but this time inside her head and inside her heart.

"Zac." She couldn't stop kissing him. The Carmia public-works department would find them still like this in the morning.

"Chris." He apparently couldn't stop kissing her, either. By Wednesday they'd be dead of thirst.

"You and I are going to stay together." He wasn't asking. He was really hers, this man who'd stop at nothing. "Whether I have to bribe my way into Columbia or get a job selling tokens in the subway, I am not letting you go."

"Oh, Zac." Chris gave a half laugh, half sob of happiness. "That's fine. Really."

"No, seriously. I am not letting you go. We will have to find ways to work and shower and eat wrapped around each other like this."

"Okay." The sobs gave way to pure giggles. "That is totally fine with me."

He leaned his forehead against hers. "Oh, Chris. I can't believe how close I came to letting you go."

"Oh, Zac." She lifted her hand to touch his cheek. "I can't believe how close I came to going."

"You know what?" He lifted his head and grinned at her. "From now on I would *much* rather hear you say you are close to coming."

"Mmm, that *does* sound better." She moved provocatively against him. "Speaking of which…"

"My place or yours?"

"Doesn't matter. Because wherever we go, it will be you and me." She kissed him, her love, her future, the man who had helped her become the woman she wanted to be, by uncovering the woman she'd been all along. "And nothing in any place or in any city can change that."

Epilogue

"I NOW PRONOUNCE you husband and wife."

Bodie turned to Gail, who looked so hot in her black leather wedding dress that he wanted the damn ceremony over with so he could get her back into bed.

He hadn't expected to fall in love with her. Hell, he never thought he was the love-forever type. But she kept him coming back for more and more and more, and then one day he just felt like proposing, so he did.

They bought a house on the beach in Encinitas, just north of San Diego, the quintessential surf town. Maybe he'd get Gail to pop out a few kids. That would be cool. He owed it to the world to pass along the big bad Bodie DNA to some cranking little surfer-dudes.

"You may kiss the bride."

He kissed his wife, wincing when she bit his tongue hard. She'd pay for that. Then she'd make him pay for what he did. And on and on into their happy ever after.

Life was kicking ass.

"I NOW PRONOUNCE you husband and wife."

Gus started crying. He couldn't help it. Pammy was so beautiful in her white gown, with the big poufy veil.

He was the luckiest guy in the world. And she didn't do too badly, either.

He was winning tournaments now and then, instead of just placing, pretty sure he was heading for the big time, but he worried that with a wife now and kids someday, maybe he better get serious about a career. He could always...

Or maybe he'd be good at ...

Uh.

He was a surfer. What could he say?

Pammy was studying to be an X-ray technician. Practically a doctor. She was so smart. He was away from home more than he wanted, but it was so much more special now coming back to Carmia than it had ever been, with this perfect woman waiting for him.

"You may kiss the bride."

Yeah, he was all over that. And looking forward to doing it every day until death.

Life had totally worked out.

"I NOW PRONOUNCE you husband and wife."

Summer smiled up at Luke, letting him see all the love in her eyes. He looked so gorgeous! He no longer wore the brow ring, and he'd cut his hair shorter. It made him look older and *so* sexy. Women were always flirting with him.

They'd made a wonderful home at Zac's, both studying full-time at Cal Poly. As planned, Summer was pursuing her dream of a psychology degree. Luke was taking on computer science and doing really well. He was serious about his studies, serious about becoming a husband and someday a father. Both of them were amazed at how easily they'd adjusted to living together. She was getting married a lot younger than she'd ever dreamed of doing, but Luke… Well, she couldn't imagine ever being without him.

"You may kiss the bride."

She kissed her new husband, beaming at him, so glad so many of their friends had been able to join them for their wedding. Even her family had behaved. They liked Luke. Who wouldn't?

Life was finally as she'd always wanted it to be, full of laughter and full of love.

"I NOW PRONOUNCE you husband and wife…and husband and wife."

Chris beamed at Zac, then peeked behind her for a quick second to beam at Eva who was facing Ames at their double wedding outside Slow Pour, under a tent, on a red carpet.

Of course Zac had gotten into Columbia—he'd gotten in practically everywhere he applied. Which was good, because she was pretty sure selling subway tokens would have gotten old fast for a guy with his brains. It was great being back in the city of all cities, but she'd missed Carmia more than she expected. Zac had taken to Manhattan well for the most part. Winter, not so much. After he graduated, she planned to sell NYEspresso and return here with him. She and Eva would share the ownership and management of Slow Pour, so when kids started arriving the two couples would be able to maintain a good balance between family and career.

"You may kiss the bride."

She closed her eyes and kissed her husband, concentrating on the feel of his lips, on the roar of approval around them, on the fresh sea air and the deep, deep happiness in her heart.

Life in the moment didn't get much better than this.

* * * * *

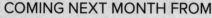

COMING NEXT MONTH FROM

Available February 17, 2015

#835 SEARCH AND SEDUCE
Uniformly Hot!
by Sara Jane Stone

This time, Amy Benton is writing the rules: no strings, no promises and definitely no soldiers. Once she sees gorgeous pararescue jumper Mark Rhodes shirtless, though, she just may break every one...

#836 UNDER THE SURFACE
SEALs of Fortune
by Kira Sinclair

Former SEAL Jackson Duchane is searching for a sunken ship full of gold. Business rival Loralei Lancaster is determined to beat him to it. The race is on—if they can stay out of bed long enough to find the treasure.

#837 ANYWHERE WITH YOU
Made in Montana
by Debbi Rawlins

Stuntman and all-around bad boy Ben Wolf is only visiting Blackfoot Falls for a few days. But Deputy Grace Hendrix makes him want to get in trouble with the law...in a whole new way!

#838 PULLED UNDER
Pleasure Before Business
by Kelli Ireland

When Harper Banks barged into his club, Levi Walsh was ready to dress her down...all the way to her lacy lingerie. Until she tells him she's an IRS investigator—and she's closing his business!

REQUEST YOUR FREE BOOKS!
2 FREE NOVELS PLUS 2 FREE GIFTS!

HARLEQUIN

Blaze®

red-hot reads!

YES! Please send me 2 FREE Harlequin® Blaze™ novels and my 2 FREE gifts (gifts are worth about $10). After receiving them, if I don't wish to receive any more books, I can return the shipping statement marked "cancel." If I don't cancel, I will receive 4 brand-new novels every month and be billed just $4.74 per book in the U.S. or $4.96 per book in Canada. That's a savings of at least 14% off the cover price. It's quite a bargain. Shipping and handling is just 50¢ per book in the U.S. and 75¢ per book in Canada.* I understand that accepting the 2 free books and gifts places me under no obligation to buy anything. I can always return a shipment and cancel at any time. Even if I never buy another book, the two free books and gifts are mine to keep forever.

150/350 HDN F4WC

Name _____ (PLEASE PRINT)

Address _____ Apt. #

City _____ State/Prov. _____ Zip/Postal Code

Signature (if under 18, a parent or guardian must sign)

Mail to the **Harlequin® Reader Service:**
IN U.S.A.: P.O. Box 1867, Buffalo, NY 14240-1867
IN CANADA: P.O. Box 609, Fort Erie, Ontario L2A 5X3

Want to try two free books from another line?
Call 1-800-873-8635 or visit www.ReaderService.com.

* Terms and prices subject to change without notice. Prices do not include applicable taxes. Sales tax applicable in N.Y. Canadian residents will be charged applicable taxes. Offer not valid in Quebec. This offer is limited to one order per household. Not valid for current subscribers to Harlequin Blaze books. All orders subject to credit approval. Credit or debit balances in a customer's account(s) may be offset by any other outstanding balance owed by or to the customer. Please allow 4 to 6 weeks for delivery. Offer available while quantities last.

Your Privacy—The Harlequin® Reader Service is committed to protecting your privacy. Our Privacy Policy is available online at www.ReaderService.com or upon request from the Harlequin Reader Service.

We make a portion of our mailing list available to reputable third parties that offer products we believe may interest you. If you prefer that we not exchange your name with third parties, or if you wish to clarify or modify your communication preferences, please visit us at www.ReaderService.com/consumerschoice or write to us at Harlequin Reader Service Preference Service, P.O. Box 9062, Buffalo, NY 14269. Include your complete name and address.

HB13R2

*Mark had been her husband's best friend. Was it wrong
to want more from him than a shoulder to cry on?*

*Read on for a sneak preview of
SEARCH AND SEDUCE,
a **UNIFORMLY HOT!** novel
by Sara Jane Stone.*

"In those first few months, I made a cup of cocoa every
night. Then I'd sit here and email you."

"You stopped sending memories of Darren," Mark
said. "About six months ago."

"You noticed." Amy lowered the mug, a line of hot
chocolate on her upper lip.

His gaze locked on her mouth. He wanted to lean
forward and kiss her lips clean.

She shrugged. "I guess I was done living in the past.
It was a good idea, though. It helped me find my way
through it all."

He stared at their joined hands. "Must have been, if
you started a new list."

Her fingers pressed against his skin. "This one's different."

"I know." He felt her drawing closer.

"I'm writing the rules this time." Her eyes lit with
excitement. Unable to look away, Mark saw the moment
desire rose up to meet her newfound joy.

He withdrew his hand. "I should go."

Mark pushed back from the table and stood. But Amy followed, stepping close, invading his space. Her hands rose, and before he could move away, he felt her palms touch his face.

He froze, not daring to move. He didn't even blink, just stared down at her. Her gaze narrowed in on his lips, her body shifting closer. Rising on to her tiptoes, she touched her lips to his.

Mark closed his eyes, his hands forming tight fists at his sides. He felt her tongue touch his lower lip as if asking for more. Unable to hold back, he gave in, opening his mouth to her kiss, deepening it, making it clear that this kiss was not tied to an offering of friendship and comfort.

Amy's hands moved over his jaw, running up through his hair. Pulling his mouth tightly against hers. He groaned. She tasted like chocolate—sweet and delicious. He wanted more, so damn much more.

Her fingers ran down the front of his shirt, moving lower and lower. His body hardened, ready and wanting.

He reached for her wrist, gently drawing her away. Then he leaned closer, his lips touching her ear, allowing her to hear the low growl of need in his voice. "Let me know when you've written your rules."

Don't miss
SEARCH AND SEDUCE by Sara Jane Stone,
available March 2015 wherever
Harlequin® Blaze® books and ebooks are sold.

www.Harlequin.com

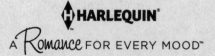